Camp Club Girls

Kate's
Vermont
VENTURE

© 2010 by Barbour Publishing, Inc.

Edited by Jeanette Littleton.

ISBN 978-1-60260-293-9

Scripture quotations marked KJV are taken from the King James Version of the Bible.

Scripture quotations marked NKJV are taken from the New King James Version®. Copyright © 1982 by Thomas Nelson, Inc. Used by permission. All rights reserved.

Cover design: Thinkpen Design

Published by Barbour Publishing, Inc., P.O. Box 719, Uhrichsville, Ohio 44683, www.barbourbooks.com

Our mission is to publish and distribute inspirational products offering exceptional value and biblical encouragement to the masses.

ecpa Member of the
Evangelical Christian
Publishers Association

Printed in the United States of America.
Dickinson Press, Grand Rapids, MI; August 2010; D10002448

Camp Club Girls

Kate's
Vermont
VENTURE

Janice Hanna

BARBOUR
PUBLISHING

Three Blind Mice

"Ahhh!" Kate Oliver screamed as she ran from the Mad River Creamery. Her heart raced a hundred miles an hour. "Wait, Sydney!"

Her friend half-turned with a frantic look on her face. She kept running, nearly slipping on the icy pavement. "We can't stop! N−not yet!"

"B−but. . .you're too fast! I can't keep up!" Kate paused to catch a few breaths. Then she ran again. The sooner she could get away from what she'd just seen. . .the better!

From behind, she heard others crying out as they ran from the building. She'd never seen so many people move so fast! Kate had a feeling none of them would ever visit the Mad River Creamery again!

Whoosh! Kate's feet hit the slippery patch of ice. She began to slip and slide all over the place.

"Nooooooo!" she hollered as her tennis shoes sailed out from underneath her. She slid a few more feet, finally plopping onto her bottom on the icy pavement. Her tiny video camera flew up in the air. Thankfully Kate caught it before it hit the ground. When she screamed, Sydney finally stopped running and turned around.

"What are you doing?" her friend asked, sprinting her way. "We've got to get out of here! I can't stand. . ." Sydney's voice began to shake. "I can't stand. . .*rats*!"

Kate shuddered and the memories flooded back. Not just one but *three* jumbo-sized rats had raced across the floor of the creamery during their tour. One had scampered across her toes! Kate shivered—partly from the cold Vermont air, and partly from remembering the sight of those horrible, ugly creatures! *Oh, how sick!* And—just in case no one believed them—she'd caught the whole thing on video!

Sydney's hand trembled as she helped Kate up. "Let's go, Kate. I'm never coming back here. Never!" Sydney's dark braids bobbed back and forth as she shook her head. Kate saw the fear in her friend's eyes.

"But I *have* to come back," Kate argued as she brushed ice off her backside. "My school report! We'll only be in Mad River Valley a week. I have to get it written! I'll never get an A in science if I don't finish it."

"Just choose a different topic. Your teacher won't care—especially if you tell her what happened!" Sydney said as they started walking. "Vermont has lots of great things you could write about. Why don't you write your essay on your aunt's inn? Or about the ski lifts? They're the coolest I've ever seen!"

Kate shrugged, still feeling sore from falling. "I don't

know anything about skiing, remember? You know I'm not into sports. And nothing is scientific about my aunt's inn. This is supposed to be a *science* paper not a *What I did on my Christmas vacation* essay!"

"Well then, what about the Winter Festival?" Sydney suggested. "I read about it in the paper at the inn, and I even saw a poster advertising it. They're having all sorts of races and prizes. Maybe you can write about competition from a scientific angle."

Kate groaned. "I guess, but none of that is as exciting as the creamery. I had so many ideas for my paper, and now. . ." She sighed. "Now I probably won't even get to go back in there."

"The Mad River Creamery is exciting, all right!" Sydney agreed. "Just wait till your teacher finds out about rats in their cheese! She'll tell her students and they'll tell their parents! Before long, supermarkets won't even carry Mad River Valley products anymore."

"I guess you're right," Kate said with a shrug.

Sydney laughed. "If you *do* go back, you should get extra credit for this paper, that's all I've got to say!" Her eyes lit up. "I know! Show your teacher that video! That will get you some bonus points!"

Kate sighed. "It does creep me out to think about going back in the creamery, but I wanted to write about all the electronic gizmos they use to turn milk into cheese. It's so. . . fascinating!"

"Yes," Sydney agreed, "but *rats* are not fascinating." She squeezed her eyes shut. Opening them again, she said, "They're awful, disgusting creatures! I hope I never see another one as long as I live."

Kate laughed as she trudged along on the snow-packed sidewalk. "I've never seen you scared of anything, Sydney. You're the bravest person I know."

"Just because I'm athletic doesn't mean I like rats and snakes and stuff." Sydney shook her head. "No thank you! I'll scale the highest heights. Ski down the biggest mountain. . .but don't ask me to look at a rat! Ugh!" Her hands began to tremble.

Kate looked at her friend curiously. "Why do rats scare you so much, anyway?"

Sydney's eyes widened. "I can't believe I never told you! A couple of years ago at summer sports camp, one of the boys put a mouse in my lunch sack."

"No way!"

"Yes. I opened the bag, and the rodent stared at me with his beady eyes." Sydney's voice shook. "I threw the bag halfway across the room."

"Aw." Kate giggled. "Was the mouse okay?"

"Was the *mouse* okay?" Sydney looked at her with a stunned expression. "What about me? Why aren't you asking if *I* was okay? It scared me to death! Seriously!"

"Still, it's kinda funny," Kate said, trying not to smile.

"Well, not to me. I've never liked mice. . .or *rats*. . .since.

And especially not in a creamery." Sydney shook her head. "Not that the creamery will be open for long. I'll bet the health inspector's going to come and shut the place down permanently. That's what I'd do, anyway."

"That's just so sad!" Kate sighed. "For the owners, I mean. I'd hate to be in their shoes right now!"

"Me, too!" Sydney said. "'Cause their shoes. . .and their feet. . .are still inside that awful creamery!"

Kate finally started to relax as they walked together the three blocks to her aunt and uncle's inn—the Valley View Bed and Breakfast. When they drew close to the building, Kate saw her brother Dexter outside building a snowman. "Just wait till Dex hears about the rats!"

"Hey, Dex!" Sydney hollered. "Do we have a story for you!"

The nine-year-old rose and brushed snow off his wet knees. Then he jogged toward them, his cheeks bright red from playing in the cold. "What's up?"

"We saw *rats* at the creamery!" Sydney began to tell the story with great animation. Before long, Dexter's eyes grew so wide they looked like they might pop out.

"No joke? Rats! Ooo, that's so cool!" He rubbed his hands together. "Let's go back. I want to see them. Do you think they'll let me keep one? It's been ages since I've had a pet rat!" He rattled on about how much fun it would be to share his room with a rat.

Kate shuddered. "This isn't the day to ask. They've closed the creamery for the afternoon. I bet they won't even be open tomorrow."

"And besides. . .those weren't pet rats." Sydney squeezed her eyes shut and shivered. "They're probably disease-carrying rats."

Dex scrunched up his nose and said, "Sick! Never mind, then!"

A voice rang out from the front of the inn, and Kate saw Aunt Molly at the front door, waving. Then Uncle Ollie joined her.

"Come inside, kids. Lunchtime!" Uncle Ollie hollered.

"I've made homemade vegetable soup!" Aunt Molly added. "Perfect for a cold day like this. And we have apple pie for dessert!"

"Everyone in Mad River Valley knows your Aunt Molly bakes the best apple pies around!" Uncle Ollie said with a wink.

Kate smiled at her uncle. He looked so much like her father they could almost pass for twins. Uncle Ollie was older. And mostly bald. But she still saw the family resemblance. How funny that Uncle Ollie had just married a woman named Molly! Kate still giggled, when she thought about it. Ollie and Molly Oliver. Their names just tripped across her tongue.

"Apple pie!" Dexter began to run toward the house. "My favorite!"

"Mmm!" Kate smacked her lips. Aunt Molly's great cooking would surely take her mind off of what had just happened. . .unless she served cheese on top of the pie!

Inside, Kate and Sydney pulled off their mittens and scarves, snow falling on the front rug. Kate's dog, Biscuit, jumped up and down, excited to see them. Then he licked up the little puddles of water from the melting snow.

"Sorry about the mess, Aunt Molly." Kate sighed.

"Never apologize for falling snow, honey," Aunt Molly said. "I always say snowflakes are kisses from heaven. So I don't mind a little mess. You girls have just left kisses on my floor!"

"You're so sweet." Kate hugged her aunt, noticing the familiar smell of her aunt's tea rose perfume.

"So. . ." Aunt Molly flashed a warm smile as she helped Sydney with her jacket. "What do you think of Mad River Valley? Did you kids find anything exciting in our little town?"

"Oh, more than you know!" Kate shrugged off her heavy winter coat. She explained what had happened, then added, "I don't know if I can ever look at Mad River Cheddar Cheese the same way again."

"I bet supermarkets all over the country stop selling it!" Sydney added.

Her aunt's brow wrinkled. "Oh dear! I know the Hamptons, who own the creamery. They're such nice people. This is terrible. . .terrible!"

"Very strange," Uncle Ollie added, shaking his head. "Highly unusual goings-on over there lately."

Aunt Molly led the girls into the kitchen, and Kate's parents soon joined them. After they sat down at a fully laden table and asked God to bless the food, Kate told her parents about their adventurous trip, but Sydney interrupted and told the part about the rats. "It was d–d–dis–*gus*–ting!" she added.

"Not a rat fan?" Uncle Ollie asked.

Sydney shook her head. "No, sir!"

"When Dexter was younger, he had a pet rat named Cheez-It," Kate's father explained. "I'll never forget that little guy. He was pretty cute, actually."

"Only, he bit me and I started calling him Cheez-*Nips*," her mother added, then grinned. "I never could stand rats. Still can't."

Sydney shivered, but Kate laughed. "They're okay in a cage," she said, "but not running around in a creamery."

Suddenly the food didn't look very appetizing, even to Kate, who usually loved to eat. And she couldn't help but notice the cubes of cheese in the center of the table. She closed her eyes and pretended they weren't there.

Aunt Molly clucked her tongue as she scooped up big bowls of steaming vegetable soup. "That poor, poor Hampton family. Haven't they had enough trouble already? Now their creamery will be shut down. It's a shame, I tell you."

She set a bowl of soup in front of Kate, and suddenly her appetite returned. She took a yummy bite and listened to the adults talk.

"Has this happened before?" Kate's mother asked.

"Sadly, yes," Uncle Ollie said.

"This isn't the first time the health inspectors have come," Aunt Molly explained. "They've been out twice before. Can't imagine what's causing this."

"Sounds like they'll have to shut the place down permanently, then," Kate's dad said.

Aunt Molly shook her head. "Just seems so sad. I've known the Hamptons since I was young. They're good people. And the creamery has had such a great record of cleanliness. Until a week ago. First I heard about an ant infestation. Then spiders. And now. . .rats! This is all so. . .shocking. Folks around here just find this all so unbelievable!"

"Hmm." Kate pondered her aunt's words. "Why *would* they have a rat problem now, after all these years? Out of the blue? Seems. . ."

"Suspicious?" Sydney whispered.

"Yes."

"Highly unusual goings-on," her uncle added, shaking his head. "Quite odd."

Kate looked at Sydney, her excitement growing. "Are you saying what I *think* you're saying?"

"Maybe they don't *really* have a rat problem at the creamery," Sydney whispered. "Maybe someone is just trying to make it *look* like they do, to sabotage them!"

"But, why?" Kate asked. "And what can we do about it?"

"I'm not sure, but I'm gonna pray about it." Sydney nodded.

"Me, too. And maybe, just maybe. . ." Kate smiled, thinking about the possibilities. This wouldn't be the first case she and Sydney had solved together. No, with the help of their friends—the Camp Club Girls—they'd almost become super-sleuths! They even had a page on the Internet and a chat room!

"I'm glad you're going to help figure this out," Dex said with a frantic look in his eyes. "If the Mad River Creamery shuts down, I won't be able to eat my favorite cookies 'n' cream ice cream anymore!"

"Oh, that's right." Kate clamped her hand over her mouth. "It's not just the cheese customers will be losing. . . it's ice cream, too."

"And milk," her mother added. "Their milk is the best in the country."

"But I'll miss their ice cream most," Dexter said with a pout.

Kate forced a serious expression as she said, "Especially their newest flavor."

"Newest flavor?" Sydney and Dexter looked at her with curious looks on their faces.

"Rat-a-tat-tat!" She almost fell off of the chair, laughing. "Get it? *Rat*-a-tat-tat!" She doubled over with laughter.

"That's horrible, Kate Oliver!" Sydney said, standing. "I'm never going to be able to enjoy ice cream again."

"You don't eat sugar anyway," Kate said with a shrug. "You're the healthiest person I know. But me. . ." She sighed. It really would be tough for her to give up Mad River's famous ice cream.

But how could she eat it now, knowing they had a. . .what would you call it? A vermin problem. That's what they had: vermin. Vermin in Vermont.

"Ugh!" A shiver ran down her spine. Vermin in Vermont. Would she ever think of the state again without thinking of. . .rats?

Only if they solved the case!

I Smell a Rat

After lunch, the girls took Biscuit for a walk and talked about the case.

"I wonder if this is a case of sabotage," Kate said, kicking up a pile of snow with her boot. "I think so. Don't you think?"

"Probably if they've had so many problems they've never had before. But, why?" Sydney asked, looking worried.

Kate sighed as she pulled her coat tighter to fight off the bitter cold. "We need to call the other Camp Club girls. Surely one of them would know what to do."

Sydney giggled. "Knowing Bailey, she would also want to fly out here and join us."

Kate laughed. "Yes, and Alexis would be telling us just how much this case is like some book she read, or some movie she watched."

"Elizabeth would remind us to pray, of course," Sydney added. "And to guard what we say so that we don't falsely accuse anyone."

"Yes, and she'd probably quote that scripture she loves

so much. . .'Vengeance is mine; . . .saith the Lord.'" Kate smiled, just thinking about her friend. Elizabeth loved the Lord so much, and it showed in everything she said and did.

"What about McKenzie?" Sydney asked.

"She would keep searching for clues till she found the culprit!" Kate explained. "You know McKenzie! She would examine the motives of every suspect until she solved the case."

"Can we call a meeting of the Camp Club Girls in our chat room tonight?" Sydney asked. "Does the inn have Internet access?"

"Uncle Ollie has a wireless router," Kate said. "I know, because I've already checked my e-mail on my wristwatch."

"Your wristwatch?" Sydney looked at her curiously.

"Yes, remember?" Kate stopped walking long enough to hold up her watch. "I have an Internet wristwatch. One of my dad's students at Penn State invented it. He's a robotics professor, you know."

"I know, I know." Sydney laughed. "And you're going to be one when you grow up, too!"

"Yep," Kate agreed. She looked at her watch once more. "I have to be close to a wireless signal to get online on my wristwatch," she explained. "We're too far from the house now or I'd show you how it works."

Sydney grinned. "Okay, Inspector Gadget! I always forget you've got such cool stuff."

Kate laughed when Sydney called her by the familiar

funny nickname. "Well, that's what happens when your dad is into electronics like mine is! He gives me all of his old stuff—cell phones, digital recorders, mini-cams, and all that kind of stuff—when one of his students invents something better. And this watch. . ." She glanced down at it with a smile. "It's the coolest gadget of all. I can check my webmail and even send instant messages with it."

"And check the time, too!" Sydney chuckled. "Which is about all I can do on my watch. . .period!"

"Speaking of the time, I think it's nearly time to meet Uncle Ollie and Dad in the big red barn out back." Kate squinted to catch a glimpse of the building through the haze of the drifting snow. "They're in the workshop."

"Why are we meeting them, again?" Sydney asked.

"I think Uncle Ollie wants to introduce us to someone. There's a neighborhood boy who's been helping him with some of his projects. I think his name is Michael. We're supposed to be nice to him." She shrugged, unsure of what to say next.

"Is he cute?" Sydney asked with a twinkle in her eye.

Kate shrugged. "I don't know. Could be. I just know that Uncle Ollie said he's kind of a loner." She shivered against a suddenly cold wind that tossed some loose snow in her face.

"A loner?" Sydney wrinkled her nose. "Meaning, he doesn't have any friends? That's kind of weird."

"Maybe." Kate sighed. "Molly told me he's just sad because his grandfather died last month. So Uncle Ollie's been playing a grandfatherly role in his life. I think that's pretty nice, actually."

"Oh, I see." Sydney looped her arm through Kate's. "Well, why didn't you just say so? I'll be extra-nice to him. Poor guy."

With Biscuit on their heels, the girls trudged through the now-thick snow to get to the barn. Kate pulled back the door, amazed at what she found inside.

"Doesn't look like any barn I've ever seen!" Sydney said with a look of wonder on her face.

"I know." They stood for a moment, just taking in the sights. "Look at all of Uncle Ollie's electronics! This place is even better than my dad's workshop in our basement."

"I can sure tell your dad and his brother are related!" Sydney said.

"No kidding. Except, of course, Uncle Ollie is a lot older. And he is so smart!" Why, next to Dad, he was the smartest man Kate had ever met.

Off in the distance they heard voices. Kate followed them until they reached a small, crowded work space filled with all sorts of electronics and robotic goodies. "There you are!" she said as she caught a glimpse of her father and uncle.

A boy, about fourteen, stood in the distance. *That must be Michael.* He was tall and thin with messy hair that needed to be combed.

Michael turned to look at them with a nervous look on

his face. At once, Biscuit began to growl.

How odd, Kate thought. *Biscuit gets along with everyone!*

"Stop it, Biscuit!" She tugged his leash and he stopped, but she could tell Biscuit was still uneasy. Very, very unusual. Something about this boy made Kate suspicious right away. She immediately scolded herself. *Stop it, Kate. He's never done anything to you. Be careful not to pass judgment on someone you don't even know!*

Sydney didn't seem to notice the tension in the air. She went right up to Michael and introduced herself with a welcoming smile. After taking a seat on a nearby chair, she asked, "Have you lived in the area long?"

He shrugged, but never looked her way. "I grew up in Mad River Valley. Why?"

"Oh, I just wondered." She looked around the workshop then glanced back his way. "Do you ski?"

"Of course. Who doesn't?" He looked at her as if she were crazy.

"I don't," Kate said. "Never have."

He shrugged and went back to working on some electronic contraption. "That's weird."

"So, if you ski, are you going to enter the Winter Competition?" Sydney asked.

"Maybe." He kept his eyes on his work. "I usually do, but I don't know if I feel like it this year."

"Oh, you should! It would do you good." Uncle Ollie

patted Michael on the back then turned to the girls. "You should see him ski! He's the best in his age group. Wins every year."

"Humph." Sydney crossed her arms at her chest and looked him in the eye. "We'll just see about that."

"Oh yeah?" Michael turned her way. "What do you mean by that?"

"I mean, this year *I'm* entering, too." Sydney nodded, as if that settled the whole thing.

"You are?" Kate turned to her friend, stunned. "Really?"

"Did you see the grand prize?" Sydney said, her voice growing more animated by the moment. "Three hundred dollars! That's exactly the amount I need to go on my mission trip to Mexico this summer."

"Oh, I see." Kate pondered that for a moment. Sydney would have a wonderful time on a mission trip. And Mexico. . .of all places! Sounded exciting.

Sydney sighed. "My mom doesn't make a lot of money." She shook her head. "And things are really tight right now. But she told me I could go if I could raise the money on my own. So, that's why I have to win that competition! I've read the article in the paper a dozen times at least. And I've stared at the poster in the front room of the inn a hundred times!"

"You have?" Kate looked at her, stunned. "Why didn't you say something sooner?"

"I don't know." Sydney looked down at the ground. "I

still have to come up with the entrance fee. Twenty-five dollars. But I think my mom will send it if I ask."

"Wow." Kate stared at her friend. "So you really want to do this."

"I do."

Michael crossed his arms at his chest and stared at her. "Well, maybe I *will* enter after all. We'll just see who's the best."

"Fine." Sydney shrugged. She stuck out her hand and added, "And may the best skier win!"

Michael shook her hand then went back to his work. Kate could see now that he was putting together an electronic resistor board. *What are they building out here, anyway?* she wondered. She drew near to Sydney and whispered, "What can I do to help you win the competition?"

"Hmm." Sydney pursed her lips and squinted her eyes. "I guess you could help me find the perfect skis. I'll have to rent them, probably." A sad look came over her. "I guess that will cost even more money, so maybe not. I don't know."

"Maybe Aunt Molly can help with that," Kate suggested.

"Maybe. And then I have to find out where the competition will be held. I want to hit the slopes in advance. Get in plenty of practice." Sydney's eyes lit up. "Oh, you need to come with me!"

"Me? Put on skis? I don't know. . ." Kate hesitated. "I never. . ."

"I know you've never skied before, but there's a first time for everything. Besides, I need someone to clock my time. So you won't really be doing a lot of skiing. I think it will be good for you, Kate! You'll learn something new, and I know you love learning things."

"Maybe." Kate shrugged. "Just usually not sports! But first let's go talk to Aunt Molly and see if she knows where we can get some skis."

"Hope she has two pairs!" Sydney said, looping her arm through Kate's. "Then it'll be you and me. . .off to ski!"

Another shiver ran down Kate's spine. This one had nothing to do with the cold. How could she possibly make Sydney understand. . .she didn't like sports! Not one little bit! And the very idea of soaring down a hill with boards strapped to her feet scared her half to death!

Sighing, she headed back toward the house to ask Aunt Molly about the skis. Hopefully she would only have one pair!

The Mousetrap

Kate and Sydney tromped through the snow, finally reaching the back door of the inn, which led straight into Aunt Molly's spacious kitchen with its big, roaring fireplace. As they stomped their snow-covered boots on the mat, Biscuit jumped up and down excitedly. Must be the smell of gingerbread that had him so excited!

"Oh, yum!" Kate looked down at a large tray where several cookies were cooling. "I love these!" She pulled off her coat and hung it on the coatrack, then turned to her aunt with a "Can I have one?" grin.

"I'm glad to hear that you like gingerbread." Aunt Molly handed each of the girls a warm cookie. "Taste and see if they're any good."

"Oh, they're the best I've ever had!" Kate spoke between bites. She snapped off a little piece and handed it to Biscuit, who gobbled it up and begged for more.

"I saw that, Kate!" Aunt Molly said. "You shouldn't be giving sweets to a dog!"

"I know, I know." She sighed and pulled off her mittens.

"I know I spoil him. . .way too much! But he's such a good dog, and he's been great at crime-solving, so every now and again I like to treat him."

"Treat him too much and he'll be as big around as a turkey at Thanksgiving!" Aunt Molly laughed.

"I know, I know." Kate hung her head in shame, then looked up with a grin.

"I've got some good news!" Aunt Molly said as they nibbled. "The creamery is open again. The health inspector came this morning and couldn't find any rats. In fact, they couldn't even find a hint that there had ever *been* rats. Strange, isn't it?"

"Wow! That's amazing," Kate said. "I need to go back for the tour and get some more information for my essay. Do you think Mr. Hampton would give me an interview? Maybe on video? I'd love to share it with my class. My teacher might even give me extra credit!"

"I'll call him and ask," Molly said. "Surely he will do it for me. I'm an old friend." She winked as she said the word "old" and Kate grinned.

"Do we have to go back there?" Sydney asked, looking worried. "I don't care what the health inspector said. We just saw rats in that place yesterday. Besides, I need to go skiing. I need the practice, remember?"

"Yeah." Kate leaned her elbows on the counter and sighed.

"What's wrong, Kate?" Her aunt gave her a curious look.

"Sydney wants to enter the ski competition at the

Winter Festival to raise money for a mission trip to Mexico," she explained.

"Well, that's a lovely idea!" Aunt Molly stopped working long enough to grin at Sydney. "I think that's wonderful." She set two steaming mugs of hot apple cider down in front of the girls.

"Only one problem. Well, two, actually." Sydney shrugged. "I don't have any skis, and I don't have money to enter the competition. At least, not yet. I'm going to ask my mom."

"I can help with the skis. I have a wonderful pair," Aunt Molly said with a wink. "They're in the barn. Want to go see them?"

"Well, um. . ." Sydney looked a little embarrassed.

"What, honey?"

"Well, Michael is out there, and he's going to be competing against me," she explained. "So I don't really want him to see what I'm up to."

"Oh, I see!" Aunt Molly giggled. "So this is a covert operation, then?"

"Covert operation?" Kate looked at her, confused.

"Top secret mission," Aunt Molly explained. "Is that what this is?"

"Oh yes!" Kate and Sydney spoke together.

"We don't want anyone to know anything!" Sydney explained.

"Excellent idea." Aunt Molly nodded. "And I've got just the pair of skis for you. I used to ski a little, myself. These were mine from years ago. And I've even got an extra pair for you, Kate. They're not the new, expensive kind, but they will do for a beginner."

"Oh no!" Kate argued. "I don't ski, Aunt Mol. Seriously. Not ever. And I don't want to start!"

"Hmm. Well, we'll see about that." Aunt Molly snapped the leg off a gingerbread man and popped it into her mouth. "We will just see about *that*." Biscuit stood at her side whimpering until she finally gave him a tiny piece of the cookie. "Go away, goofy dog! You're going to eat me out of house and home!"

Kate looked at Sydney, hoping to convince her. "I don't mind if you go, of course. You need the practice. I don't. And maybe I can go with you tomorrow. Today I need to stay here and research cheese-making for my essay paper."

Sydney rolled her eyes. "C'mon. Are you serious? You want me to believe you'd rather work on a school paper than hang out on the slopes?"

"You don't understand." A lump rose up in Kate's throat. "I *have* to get the best grade in the class because. . ." She didn't finish the sentence. No telling what Sydney and Aunt Molly would say if they knew the truth.

"Tell me, Kate." Sydney took another bite of a gingerbread man. "Why do you have to have the best one in your class? Why is it so important?"

"Because. . ." She shook her head. "Never mind. It's no big deal."

"Must be," Aunt Molly said, her eyes narrowing a bit. "Or you wouldn't have brought it up. Go ahead and tell us, Kate. Confession is good for the soul."

"Oh, okay." She bit her lip, trying to decide where to start. Surely Aunt Molly would understand. "There's this boy in my science class," Kate said, finally. "His name is Phillip. He's the smartest person I know."

"Smarter than you?" Sydney's eyes widened. "Impossible!"

Kate shrugged. "I don't know. Maybe. But we're always competing to see who gets the best grades. Kind of like you and Michael are going to do on the ski slopes. Lately, Phillip has been, well. . ." Her voice trailed off and she sighed.

"He's been getting better grades than you?" Aunt Molly asked.

"Yes, but that's not all." A lump rose in Kate's throat as she remembered the things Phillip had said. "He made fun of my last science project. I did a great job on it, and the teacher really liked it, but. . ."

"Oh, honey. I'm sorry he hurt your feelings." Aunt Molly shook her head.

"I don't like to be made fun of."

"No one does," Aunt Molly explained with a sympathetic look on her face.

"He doesn't sound like a very nice guy," Sydney said.

"He's not. He even told me. . ." Kate felt the anger return as she thought about him laughing at her. "He even told me that I would never be a professor like my dad. . .because I'm a girl."

"Ah." Aunt Molly nodded and handed her another cookie. "So, you're going to try to prove him wrong by being better than him at something."

"M—maybe." She shrugged and bit off the gingerbread man's head. The yummy, warm cookie slowly dissolved in her mouth.

"Kate." Aunt Molly reached over and placed her hand gently on Kate's. "It's not wrong to want to be the best you can be. But in this case, I question your motives. You've got to examine your heart, honey."

"Examine my heart?" Kate swallowed a nibble of the cookie and took a drink of the hot apple cider. "What do you mean?"

"I mean, you need to start by forgiving Phillip for what he said."

"Oh." Kate sighed and took another sip of the cider. "I never thought about that."

"Holding a grudge isn't a good thing. Besides, the Bible says the Lord will only forgive us to the extent that we forgive others."

"W—wait. What do you mean?" Kate stared at her aunt, stunned. "You mean God won't forgive me if I don't forgive Phillip?"

"Well, Ephesians 4:32 says we should be compassionate and understanding toward others, forgiving one another quickly as God forgives us."

"Whoa." Sydney and Kate both spoke at the same time.

"Forgive quickly? But that's hard to do." Kate drew in a deep breath as she thought about it. "Sometimes it takes a while to forgive, doesn't it?"

"Sometimes. But here's the problem with holding a grudge," Aunt Molly said. "It might start out small—like competing over whose essay is best. Then before you know it, a grudge can turn into revenge. Anger. And that's never good. So, it's better to put out that spark before it becomes a raging fire."

"Wow." Kate thought about her aunt's words as she continued to nibble on the cookie. It was all starting to make sense.

"Think of it like this." Aunt Molly appeared to be deep in thought for a moment. "Let's use what's going on at the creamery to illustrate. Imagine you're a little mouse and you see what looks like a beautiful piece of cheese. You run over to it and grab it, then. . .*snap!* You're caught in a mousetrap."

Kate nodded, "I see what you mean."

"Unforgiveness is a trap," Aunt Molly explained. "And as soon as you're caught in it, you're in trouble. So, let go. Forgive. It's always the best choice."

Kate stared at the fireplace, listening to the crackling and popping sounds the fire made. "I never thought about that before, Aunt Molly. I guess I have been holding a grudge but didn't realize it. Will God forgive me for that?"

"Of course He will! But you have to pray about it. And then—while you're at it—pray for Phillip, too," her aunt said. "And you never know. . .you two might end up being friends when all is said and done."

"I can't imagine that." How could she ever be a friend to such a mean person?

"I know it seems impossible now, but trust me when I say it is possible." After a wink, Aunt Molly added, "Ask me how I know."

"How do you know?" Kate asked, nibbling on her cookie.

"Because your Uncle Ollie and I met when we were competing against each other in a square-dancing competition. We were both mighty good, though maybe I shouldn't say that."

"Oh, wow!" Kate giggled. "So, who won? You or Uncle Ollie?"

"In the long run, we *both* won," Aunt Molly explained with a sly grin. "Though it certainly didn't seem like it at the time. In the second round of the competition, my partner hurt his leg. And Ollie's partner got sick. So, we ended up competing together. . .as a team." She giggled. "And the rest is history!"

Sydney's eyes sparkled. "You fell in love on the dance floor? He danced his way into your heart?"

"Well, not that first day, but it didn't take long." Aunt Molly winked. "Ollie Oliver is a godly man and a great dancer. What a charmer!" Her cheeks turned pink, and she giggled.

Sydney sighed. "That's so sweet!" She grinned at Kate. "So maybe you and Phillip will fall in love and get married someday!"

Kate shook her head. "No way! But maybe we will end up as friends like Aunt Molly said. I just never thought about it before."

Sydney nodded. "And who knows? Maybe I'll even learn to like Michael." She shrugged. "It's possible."

"I hope so," Aunt Molly said. "That would be nice. He's such a great boy."

"Hmm." Kate wrinkled her nose. "I guess we need to give him the benefit of the doubt, even though he didn't make a very good first impression."

"I still plan to beat him in the skiing competition," Sydney said. "And I do need to practice. But I'll make you a deal, Kate. Today I'll go back to the creamery with you *one* last time. But tomorrow, you have to come skiing with me. Promise?"

Kate paused. She didn't know if she should promise such a thing or not. After all, she'd never skied before. "I—I guess so," she said, finally. "But for now, let's get back to cheese-making!"

Sydney made another face then shuddered. "I sure hope there aren't any rats this time."

"Surely not," Aunt Molly said. "But if you *do* happen

to see one, just remember that story I told you about the mousetrap. It's better to forgive than hold a grudge."

"It's better to forgive than hold a grudge," Kate agreed. Then, with a happy heart, she looped her arm through Sydney's and they headed back to the creamery.

CHAPTER 4

The Big Cheese

Kate and Sydney walked the three blocks to the creamery with snow falling all around them.

"Don't you just love Vermont?" Sydney asked. "It's so pretty here." She began to describe the beautiful trees and the crystal-like snowflakes. On and on she went, sounding like a commercial.

"Mm-hmm. I like it here, but it's so cold!" Kate shivered.

"It's cold in Philly, where you live," Sydney said. "And in D.C., where I live, it gets really cold in the wintertime. So, this doesn't feel any different to me. No, I love the cold weather. And I can't wait to put on skis and glide down the mountainside. Oh, it's going to be wonderful! You're going to *love* it, Kate. I promise!"

"If you say so."

As the creamery came into view, Sydney groaned. "I can't believe I offered to come back here. This place is so scary. Do we really have to go back in there?"

"We do. But maybe we'll have a better time if we think happy thoughts," Kate suggested. "We'll focus on the good things. For example, I've been saving my allowance so I can buy different cheeses to take back to my class. You can help me decide what flavors to buy. Should I get Swiss or cheddar? And if I get cheddar, which kind? There are so many, you know." She went off on a tangent, describing her favorite kinds of cheese.

"I can't believe you're actually going to *eat* something made there." Sydney scrunched her nose. "I'd be scared to! Aren't you worried?"

"Nah," Kate said, shaking her head. "And besides, I have the *strangest* feeling about all of that, Sydney. I'm convinced someone is sabotaging the Hamptons. But, why?"

"Hmm." Sydney walked in silence a moment. "Maybe we should put McKenzie or one of the other Camp Club Girls to work, figuring out who their main competitor is. Maybe someone from another creamery is jealous and wants to put the Hamptons out of business."

Just before they entered the building, Kate caught a glimpse of someone familiar off in the distance. "Hey, look, Sydney! It's that boy. . .Michael! Are you going to tell him that you're entering the competition?"

"No way!" Sydney grabbed her arm and whispered. "It's top secret, remember? I don't want him to know."

They walked inside the store at the front of the creamery, and Kate took a deep breath. "Oh, it smells so deliciously cheesy in here!" She closed her eyes and breathed in and out a few times. "I totally believe this is what heaven it going to smell like."

Sydney grunted. "Heaven. . .smells like *cheese*? I sure hope not! Doesn't smell so good to me." After looking around the empty store, she added, "Look, Kate. Have you noticed? We're the only ones here. That should tell you something! People are scared to come back."

"Or maybe we're just early." Kate looked at her Internet wristwatch. "Ooo! I have an e-mail." She quickly signed online and smiled as she read a note from Bailey that said, "Have fun in Vermont!" Kate quickly typed back, "Having a blast!" then pressed the tiny SEND button.

"I don't blame people for being scared to come here," Sydney said.

Kate looked up from her watch and shrugged. "Well, let's not think about all that. Since we're here, let's sample the cheeses."

"I guess so." Sydney shrugged. "But you can do the sampling. I'll just watch."

They walked around the large glass case, looking inside. "Oh, I *love* Colby Jack!" Kate reached for her camera and took a picture of the tray filled with chunks of orange and white swirled cheese. Then she lifted the clear dome top from the cheese tray and took a piece. With her mouth full, she pointed at the tray next to it. "They have every kind of cheddar imaginable! Yum!" She lifted the top on that tray and took several pieces. "Wow, this is great!" She'd never seen so many different kinds of cheeses. . .and all the samples were free! But which one should she buy for her classmates?

"My favorite is the Swiss," Sydney said, taking a tiny piece. "Mom puts it on my turkey sandwiches."

"Ooo, you're making me hungry." Kate took a couple of chunks of the Swiss cheese and ate it right away. "Let's order something to eat." She pointed at the Cheese-o-Rama Snack Shack in the corner of the room. "Look! It says they make the world's best grilled-cheese sandwiches, and you can pick the kind of cheese you want. I'm going to ask for the Colby Jack on mine. What about you?"

"Kate, we just ate breakfast a couple of hours ago," Sydney said. "And then we ate your aunt's gingerbread cookies. I don't need the extra calories. And I still think we should be careful not to eat too much cheese from this place."

"Calories, schmalories." Kate shrugged. "Who cares?"

"I do." Sydney gave her a stern look. "I have to stay in shape to win that competition next weekend."

"You're already the fastest, strongest, most athletic girl I know!" Kate said. "What else do you want?"

"I want to win."

"Well, I'm not competing, and I'm hungry. Besides, it's almost lunchtime and we'll never make it back to the inn in time for Aunt Molly's food. So, let's eat!"

Kate went to the counter and ordered a cheese sandwich with a side of cheese-flavored chips. Mr.

Hampton—her aunt's friend—prepared her sandwich. He looked a little worried.

As he placed her plate in front of her, Kate whispered, "Mr. Hampton, did my Aunt Molly Oliver call you?"

"She did." He gave a hint of a smile.

"Could I speak with you. . .alone?" She looked around, hoping not to be overheard, then remembered no one else was in the shop. "I'm working on a paper for school and would love to get some information—straight from the source!"

"Sure, I'd be happy to help." His shoulders sagged as he looked around the shop. "Doesn't look like we've got many customers today, anyway." He sighed. "What a mess this is! We can't afford to lose customers right now."

"I understand." Kate gave him a sympathetic look. "And I want to help you with that. In my essay I'll tell everyone how wonderful your cheeses are. That should help your business! But I'll need your help. Thanks for answering a few questions for me!"

Just then, a cheerful female voice came over the loudspeaker. "Ladies and gentlemen, the Mad River Creamery will conduct a tour of its facility in exactly ten minutes. The tour is free of charge, and complimentary cheese samples will be given along the way. Join us for the tour of a lifetime."

"It's the tour of a lifetime, all right," Sydney whispered in Kate's ear as she drew near. "Complete with rats."

"Shh!" Kate ignored her and turned her attention back to Mr. Hampton. "Maybe after the tour you could answer some questions for me? I'll be sure to give you credit in my paper. And I'll need to purchase lots of different kinds of cheeses to take back for the kids in my class, so I'll need help picking those out, too."

"Of course!" he said with a smile. "I'm always happy to help a customer."

Just then, a couple more customers came through the door—a woman in a beautiful white fur coat and a man with a sour look. He shook the snow off of his leather coat and looked around the shop with a frown.

"Wow, he doesn't look happy," Sydney whispered in Kate's ear. "Do you think his wife made him come?"

"I don't know." Kate stared at the man, then turned back to her sandwich. "Maybe he heard about the rats and is afraid."

"He doesn't look like the kind of man to be scared of anything. He just looks. . .mean." A look of fear came into Sydney's eyes. "I hope they're not coming on the tour with us."

The woman walked toward them and the man followed closely behind, muttering all the way.

"Uh-oh." Kate let out a nervous giggle. "Looks like they're joining us. Just smile and be friendly. Maybe they'll turn out to be nice."

"Whatever you say," Sydney whispered.

Within seconds, Kate and Sydney were tagging along

behind Mr. Hampton and the two strangers into the creamery. She couldn't get rid of the nagging feeling that the man and woman were up to no good. And Sydney made her a little nervous. She wouldn't stop talking about rats.

"I can't believe I'm doing this again!" Sydney whispered. "I still have vermin-phobia after our last tour!"

"Shh." Kate turned and gave her a *please-be-quiet* look.

The girls walked from room to room, listening as Mr. Hampton explained the process of cheese making. Kate pulled out her video camera and began to film his presentation. In one room, he pointed out something he called curds and whey.

"Just like Little Miss Muffett," Kate whispered.

"What?" Sydney gave her a funny look.

"'Little Miss Muffett sat on her tuffet, eating her curds and whey.'" Kate giggled. "Now I know what curds and whey are. I never knew before. Kind of looks like cottage cheese. Kind of chunky and. . ." *Gross* was the only word that came to mind, but she didn't say it.

"Doesn't look very appetizing!" Sydney made a terrible face. "It's enough to scare me away, too!"

"Well, in the nursery rhyme, a *spider* frightened Miss Muffett away," Sydney reminded her. "Not the curds and whey. And certainly not a. . .well, a you-know-what."

Mr. Hampton turned and gave her a warning look. He put a finger over his lips, then whispered, "Don't even use the *r-a-t* word. And please don't talk about spiders, either.

I'm having enough trouble keeping my customers without worrying them even more!" He nodded in the direction of the man and woman, who stood on the other side of the room, looking at the big machine that held the curds and whey.

Kate apologized, then added, "I'm sure your customers won't be gone for long. You have the best cheese in the state, Mr. Hampton. My mom has bought Mad River Valley Cheddar for as long as I can remember." Kate raised her voice to make sure the man and woman heard her. Sure enough, the woman looked her way. "I love, love, love cheese!" She licked her lips. "Without Mad River cheese, grilled cheese sandwiches wouldn't be the same!"

"Cheeseburgers wouldn't be as cheesy!" Mr. Hampton threw in.

"String cheese wouldn't be as. . .stringy," Sydney added, then giggled.

The woman in the white coat moved their way and nodded as she said, "Cream cheese wouldn't be as creamy."

Kate turned to the man, who crossed his arms at his chest and remained quiet. Hmm. So, he didn't want to play along.

Kate decided to change the subject. "This cheese-making stuff looks like fun. I wish I could make cheese at home," she said with a sigh.

"Why, you can!" Mr. Hampton said. "If you have a gallon of milk, you can make a pound of cheese. You would need the help of a parent—and it takes a couple of days—but it's worth it. I can show you how to make your own cheese press, if you like."

"Would you, really?" Kate grew more excited by the moment. "Oh, I would love that. I think I'll write my paper on that, then!"

"Let's finish the tour, and then I'll show you a homemade cheese press," Mr. Hampton said. He led the way into a large room with a huge rectangular contraption filled with what looked like thick milk.

Kate looked at it, amazed. "Wow, this is huge." She'd never seen such a thing!

Mr. Hampton explained. "Yes, this is just like we talked about earlier. Once the whey is removed, the curds are pressed together, forming the cheese into shapes."

"Wow!" Kate began to videotape the process. She didn't want to miss a thing. Something caused her to turn toward the woman in the white coat. She was whispering something to the man and pointing to the curds and whey. *Hmm, I wonder what they're talking about?*

Just then Kate saw something out of the corner of her eye. She turned her camera toward the floor, just to make sure she wasn't imagining it. At that very moment, Sydney screamed. Kate jolted and almost dropped the camera.

"It's a. . .a rat!" Sydney jumped on a chair and began to squeal.

Sure enough, the brown furry critter headed right for

them! He was moving so fast Kate could hardly keep up with him. For a few seconds he disappeared from view in her video camera lens, and then she caught a glimpse of him again. *Oh, gross!*

The woman began to scream at the top of her lungs and fainted. Her husband caught her just before she landed on the floor. He fanned her with the creamery brochure and called, "Abigail! Abby, wake up!"

The rat scampered close to the woman and Kate gasped. *What's going to happen next?* She whispered a quick prayer.

Holding a tight grip on the camera, Kate continued videotaping the vermin. Thankfully, he scurried to the other side of the room, leaving the woman alone. But something about the little critter seemed. . .odd. It ran in circles. Round and round it went, in a never-ending cycle. Maybe it had had too much cheese! Something was definitely wrong with it.

Mr. Hampton came around to their side of the room and his eyes grew large. "No! Not again! We took care of this. I promise! Mad River Valley Creamery doesn't have. . ." He didn't say the word. He didn't have to.

The rat finally stopped running in circles and took off under the vat of cheese. The woman regained consciousness, and Kate turned her camera in that direction. The woman began to cry out and her husband hollered, "Turn that off! I don't want you videotaping my wife!"

"Oh, I'm sorry, sir. I didn't mean any harm." Tears sprang to Kate's eyes. The man headed her way. When he got close, he grabbed her camera and shut it off, then pressed it back into her hand.

"Get on out of here, kids. . .before I lose my temper. Or maybe I'll just call the police and tell them we were being illegally videotaped!"

Sydney turned on her heels and sprinted like an Olympic track star toward the door. Kate followed, shaking like a leaf.

What a mean man! She never meant to do anything wrong! And how awful. . .to see another rat! Kate couldn't figure out why, but something about that fuzzy little creature still puzzled her.

"I'm never. . .eating. . .cheese. . .again. . .as long. . .as I . . .live!" Sydney hollered as she ran.

Kate groaned, trying to keep up. So much for helping Mr. Hampton and the Mad River Creamery. Another rat had interrupted her plans. But who was behind all of this? And why?

With the help of the other Camp Club Girls. . .she and Sydney would figure it out!

Hickory Dickory Dock

Kate and Sydney ran all the way back to the inn. When they arrived at the front door, Biscuit greeted them with wet, slobbery kisses.

"D—down, boy!" Kate panted. "N—not right now."

Between the cold air and the excitement of what had just happened, she could hardly breathe!

"Is everything okay?" Aunt Molly met them as they raced into the big room. Kate headed toward the fireplace to warm herself. "N—no," she said through chattering teeth. "We saw another r—rat!"

"Oh dear, oh dear!" Aunt Molly's cheeks flushed pink. "That's just awful! Was it inside the creamery again?"

"Y—yes!"

"Oh, how terrible!" Aunt Molly began to fan herself, looking as if she might be sick.

Kate's mother entered the room with a worried look.

"Did I hear you say something about a rat?" When Kate nodded, she said, "Honey, I don't want you and Sydney going back to that creamery. You'll just have to write your essay paper on something else, Kate."

"But that's just it." Kate sighed and plopped down on the large leather chair in front of the fireplace. "It's not dangerous at all. Something is definitely up. I can feel it in my bones!"

Aunt Molly laughed. "Oh, you can, can you? Well, what do you feel?"

"I'll know more after I look at the videotape. Do you mind if I hook my camera into your big-screen TV, Aunt Molly? I want to see everything close up."

"Ugh!" Sydney grunted. "We have to see the rat on the big screen?"

Kate laughed. "You don't have to watch."

They gathered around the television as Kate hooked up her camera. When she hit PLAY, they all watched the action.

"Here's the curds and whey part," Kate explained, pointing at the screen. "And here's the part where—"

Her mother and Aunt Molly screamed when they saw the rat run across the floor toward the woman in the white coat.

"Oh, how awful!" Aunt Molly clasped her hand over her mouth. "That poor woman."

"That man who's with her looks really angry," Kate's mother added.

"Oh, he was." Kate shivered. "But look at this."

She paused the video for a moment, focusing on the rat.

"What?" Sydney drew near, looking at the television.

Kate pointed at the pesky vermin. "Take a good look at this rat."

"Do I have to?" Sydney squeezed her eyes shut. "What about him?"

"Something about him is. . .odd. First, he's a little too big. Not your average-sized rat. Not even close!"

"Well, on your Uncle Ollie's big-screen TV, everything looks bigger than it is," Aunt Molly explained.

"Yes! Look at my ears!" Sydney laughed. "They're huge. Someone please tell me they're not that big in real life!"

"They're not, silly!" Kate groaned. "I know things appear larger than they are, but even so, this is one giant rat. And look at his fur. Have you ever seen rat fur so. . .furry?"

Sydney came a step closer and looked for a second. "No. But I'm no expert on rats."

"I've seen a few in my day," Aunt Molly said, drawing close. "And he does look a bit odd. Must be an interesting species."

"I know what it is!" Sydney said. "The rats at the creamery are well fed! That's why they're so huge!"

"Could be," Kate's mother said. "I just know we don't grow them that big in Pennsylvania!"

"Or in DC!" Sydney added.

"Most rats have really short hair," Kate observed. "And most aren't this color. This is more like the fur you'd see on a hamster or something."

"So, you think it's not a rat after all?" Sydney asked.

"Maybe it's a giant hamster?"

"That's just it." She drew in a deep breath as she thought about it. "Hamsters are smaller than rats. I'm not sure what it is, but it's not a typical rat, that's for sure. I'll have to get on the Internet and research all different types of rodents."

"Doesn't sound like much fun to me!" Sydney said. "We're on Christmas vacation, Kate. Remember?"

"I know, but this is really going to bother me if I don't figure it out!" Kate backed up the video and watched it again. With a sigh, she said, "Something about this frame really bothers me. After all, rats are very agile. This one isn't."

"Agile?" Sydney groaned. "I'm gonna have to look that one up in the dictionary, Kate. Why do you always use such big words?"

Aunt Molly laughed. "I hardly use that word myself!"

"Oh, sorry." Kate giggled. "I just meant most rats move fast and can make quick turns. This one. . ." She stared at the stilled photo again. "This one makes choppy movements. Jerky. You know what I mean?"

"Maybe he's had too much cheese." Sydney laughed. "That would do it. Once I ate too much string cheese, and I could barely move at all!"

"You should see me after I've had a big slice of cheesecake," Kate's mother said with a nod. "I just want to curl up in a chair with a good book!"

"Yeah, but this is different. He didn't look like he'd eaten too much. He was. . ." Kate couldn't think of what to say next. "He's shaped weird."

"Yeah, a little." Sydney shook her head. "But can we stop looking now? I've had enough of rat talk!"

"Right, right." After a moment's pause, Kate added, "Oh, I just had an idea!"

"What?" Sydney's brow wrinkled. "What are you thinking, Kate Oliver? What are you up to?"

"Well, I was just thinking this would be a great project for McKenzie," Kate explained. "She loves to search for clues. I'll send her a picture of this. . .creature. She can research it for us."

"Okay. That's a good idea." Sydney began to pace the room as she talked. "Let's send out an e-mail to the girls and ask them to meet us in the chat room tonight at eight o'clock our time. That will give us plenty of time to hang out with your family first. What do you think?"

"Perfect."

"In the meantime," Kate's mother said, "we're still planning to go to rent a family movie and order Chinese food. Does that sound good?"

"Great! What movie?" Kate asked.

"We thought you girls could decide," her mother said. "So be thinking about it."

"Oh, I know!" Sydney clasped her hands together. "Let's rent the Nancy Drew movie. That's one of my favorites!"

"Ooo, perfect!" Kate agreed. "That should put us in the mood for solving a mystery!"

A short time later, everyone gathered around the television to watch the movie and eat Chinese food. Kate started with a big plate of moo goo gai pan, then refilled her plate with General Tso's chicken and pepper steak. Between bites, she commented on what they were watching on Uncle Ollie's big-screen TV.

"See, Sydney! See how good Nancy is at solving crimes? See that part where she kept searching for clues, even when it seemed impossible? We've got to think like that!"

"You want to be like Nancy Drew, eh?" Her father flashed an encouraging smile. "Well, you're certainly adventurous."

"And you know a lot more about technology," Sydney added. "Back when the Nancy Drew books were written, cell phones hadn't even been invented."

"No computers, either," Kate's dad threw in. "And the Internet was unheard of!"

"Wow!" Kate could hardly imagine a time without computers and Internet. She glanced at her wristwatch, thankful for modern-day technology.

As soon as the movie ended, she glanced at the clock. "Oh, it's ten minutes till eight! Time to meet with the Camp Club Girls in our chat room!"

Sydney tagged along on her heels until they reached their room. Using her dad's laptop, Kate signed online in a flash and went to their Web site chat room.

As usual, Bailey was already there. The words, *"Hey, what's up?"* appeared on the screen.

Kate: *We need your help.*

A couple minutes later, all of the girls arrived in the chat room. After explaining what had happened at the creamery, Bailey typed, *"LOL. . .I just watched* Ratatouille! *I have rats on the brain!"*

Kate: *Oh, that is ironic! Didn't the rat in that movie work in a restaurant?*
Bailey: *Yes, he was a great chef.*
Kate: *Well, maybe the rats we saw at Mad River Creamery really want to become cheese-makers!*
Bailey: *LOL.*
McKenzie: *Somehow I don't think the rats are wanting to do anything but scare people! But it sounds more like someone is putting them up to it! What can we do to help?*
Kate: *McKenzie, I'm uploading a photo of the rat. I want you to take a good look at it and compare it to other rodent photos you find online. This is a weird-looking creature. We need to know for sure what it is.*
Bailey: *Icky!*
Kate: *Alexis, would you mind doing a little research*

online? See if you can find out any information about Mad River Creamery. See if anyone might be holding a grudge against them.

Alex: *I'll find out who their competitors are! And I'll check to see if anyone is blogging about the creamery.*

Bailey: *I'll help with that. And I'll see if any complaints have been filed against the company, or if the cheese has ever made anyone sick.*

Elizabeth: *What about me? What can I do?*

Kate: *Can you put a prayer request on our blogsite? Please let people know how much we need their prayers. Also, ask them to pray for Sydney. She's competing in a skiing competition at the Winter Festival this Saturday. If she wins, the prize money will cover the cost of her trip to Mexico this summer.*

All of the girls started chatting about Sydney's trip. When they ended, Elizabeth suggested they all pray together. She typed her prayer for all of them to see.

Lord, please show us what to do. We don't want to falsely accuse anyone. Please give us wisdom and show us who is doing this awful thing to the Hamptons. Help Kate and Sydney and keep them safe. In Jesus' Name. Amen.

As she signed off of the Internet, Kate thought, once again, about Nancy Drew and the movie they'd just watched. If Nancy could solve a crime. . .surely the Camp Club Girls could figure out who was sabotaging the Mad River Creamery!

The Rat Pack

The following morning—bright and early—Sydney came in the kitchen door, her cheeks flushed pink. She shook the snow from her jacket and pulled off her scarf. "Oh, it's beautiful out there!"

"How far did you run today?" Kate asked. Seemed like every day Sydney exercised a little more and ran a little farther!

"Only two miles." Sydney shrugged as she pulled off her scarf and gloves. "I'm out of shape. Been eating too much of your Aunt Molly's good cooking. I'm really going to have to be careful once I get back home or I'm never going to stay in tip-top shape!"

"Oh, posh!" Aunt Molly laughed. "As much as you exercise, you could stand to eat even more. Never seen anyone eat as healthy as you. Well, no one your age, anyway."

"It's important! I want to do well in the competition on Saturday." Her eyes sparkled as she added, "And you know, I want to compete in the Olympics someday, too."

"She's already been in the Junior Olympics, Aunt Molly,"

Kate explained. "Sydney is a serious athlete." She stressed the word *serious*.

"Well, that's wonderful." Aunt Molly patted her own round tummy and laughed. "I could stand to be more athletic. These days I just work out in the kitchen, not the gym."

"Cooking?" Sydney asked.

"No, *eating*!" Aunt Molly let out a laugh that brought Uncle Ollie in from the next room.

"What's so funny in here?" he asked.

"Aunt Molly is just telling us how she exercises," Kate said with a giggle.

"Aunt Molly. . .exercises?" Uncle Ollie looked at them with a funny expression, as if he didn't quite believe them.

Aunt Molly giggled and lifted a fork. "Like this." Opening her mouth, she pretended to eat. "I exercise my jaw." She closed her mouth and everyone laughed.

"I hope I'm as funny as you when I'm. . ." Kate stopped before finishing.

"When you're *old*, honey?" Aunt Molly laughed. "It's okay to say it. I'm no spring chicken."

"Did someone say something about old people in here?" Kate's father entered the room, yawning. "I'm feeling old and stiff. These cold mornings are really getting to me!"

"I could use a cup of coffee, myself," Kate's mother said, entering the room behind him. "Good morning, everyone!"

"Good morning, Mom." Kate reached over and gave her mom a huge hug. "We were just talking. . ."

"About me being old," Aunt Molly threw in. "But that's okay. I don't mind admitting it. Maybe I don't work out as often as I should, and maybe I can't ski like I used to when I was young, but I can certainly pay the entrance fee for Sydney to do so."

"W—what?" Sydney gave her a surprised look.

"That's right. I paid the twenty-five dollar entrance fee for you this morning," Aunt Molly said. "I prayed about it last night and felt a little nudge from the Lord to do it. Hope you don't mind."

"Mind? Mind? Oh, Aunt Molly!" Sydney threw her arms around Kate's aunt and gave her a warm hug. "Of course I don't mind! How can I ever thank you? My mom will be so grateful!"

"Just go out there and ski the best you've ever skied." Aunt Molly patted Sydney on the back. "But take care of yourself. It's cold out and you'll be in unfamiliar territory."

"Where do we go?" Sydney asked. "Where's the best skiing around here?"

"You need to ski the Rat," Uncle Ollie explained. "That's where the competition will take place, and it's great for skiers at every level."

"The. . .what?" Sydney looked stunned.

"The Rat," he repeated. "That's the name of the most famous ski run around these parts."

"Ooo!" Sydney let out a grunt. "Why did they have to name it *The Rat*? Of all things!"

Uncle Ollie laughed. "I see your point. But don't let the name stop you. It's a great ski run. And if you make it from the top to bottom without falling, they give you a T-shirt." He went into another room and returned a few minutes later with a brown T-shirt in his hand. "I got this one back in the eighties when my ski legs were still strong."

"Wow." Kate laughed as she looked at the shirt that said THE RAT PACK on the front. "That's really cool, Uncle Ollie."

He turned it around and showed them the picture of the rat on the back.

Sydney shuddered. "I never dreamed when I said I'd compete that I'd have to ski on. . .a rat!"

"It's just a name, honey," Aunt Molly said. "And besides, you'll never overcome your fear of rats without facing it head-on. So, if you're going to teach Kate to ski, the Rat is the perfect place."

Kate shook her head. "No thank you. No skiing for me, thanks. I'll just hang out here and work on my super-sleuth blogsite."

"Oh, come on, Kate," Sydney implored. "If I can overcome my fear of rats, you can overcome your fear of skiing! And you can work on the blogsite anytime! We're on vacation now!"

"I've been a member of the Rat Pack for years," Uncle Ollie added. "We've got to keep the tradition going in our family."

"I—if I have to." Kate trembled, just thinking about it!

"Aw, don't worry," Uncle Ollie said. "I wish I could go with you girls, but I've got a project going in my workshop. Should I send along your Aunt Molly as a chaperone?"

Aunt Molly laughed. "A great one I'd be! I'd probably tumble right down the hill."

"Well, maybe I could. . ." Kate's mother started the sentence, but didn't finish it.

"Could what, Mom?"

"Well, it's been years since I skied," her mom said, "but I'm willing to give it a try. To help Sydney out, of course."

"Woo-hoo! We're going skiing!" Sydney began to squeal, but Kate's insides suddenly felt squishy!

Less than an hour later, she and Sydney arrived at the ski lift, along with Kate's mom.

"Let's put our skis on before we go up," Sydney instructed.

Kate didn't have a clue how to do that, but with help from her mom, she got the long, skinny boards strapped onto her feet.

"Now what?" she asked. She wrapped her scarf around her neck as the cold wind sent an icy shiver down her spine.

"Now we go up!" Sydney pointed up the hill.

"And we have to go up. . .in *those*?" Kate felt sick to her stomach as she looked at the little chairs.

"Oh, it's a lot of fun," her mother said. "Something you'll never forget as long as you live."

"I'm sure you're right about that!" Kate said. Somehow

she knew this whole experience was something she would never forget!

"This is the coolest ski lift ever!" Sydney said. "Like something out of the past. It's so cute."

"Cute?" Kate shook her head. "Doesn't look cute to me. Looks scary."

She stared up at the contraption, trying to figure out how it worked. After a minute or two, she relaxed. "It's really just a pulley system, isn't it? I know how pulleys work, so we should be safe."

"See! You just have to look at this like you do one of your science experiments, Kate," her mom said. "I'll help you into a chair, then I'll be in the one right behind you."

"Let's do it the other way around," Kate implored. "You two go first and I'll follow behind you."

"No way!" Sydney laughed. "If we do that, we'll turn around and you'll still be standing on the ground. We need to make sure you actually make it to the top of the hill."

After a groan, Kate agreed. "Just help me, okay?"

"Of course."

A few seconds later, Kate was in one of the chairs, rising up, up, up into the air.

"Wow!" she hollered, her voice echoing against the backdrop of snow. "It's beautiful up here!" She looked around, mesmerized. Everything was so white. . .so perfect. "I can't believe I never did this before. It's so fun!"

She reached inside her pocket and pulled out her

tiny digital camera. Unfortunately, she quickly learned that taking photos from the air—especially when the ground was covered in glistening white snow—was almost blinding! She put the camera away and held on for dear life.

When they reached the top of the hill, Kate carefully scooted off of the chair, doing her best not to fall as the skis slipped and slid underneath her. It was so hard to balance!

"Now what?" she asked, as Sydney's feet hit the ground.

Her friend offered a playful grin. "*Now* your mom and I teach you how to ski."

"I can't promise I'll be a very good teacher," Kate's mom said, looking down the hill. "It's been awhile since I've done this. Skiing is a little scary for me, too! I'm pretty wobbly!"

"I'm sure we can teach Kate what she needs to learn to make it from the top of the hill to the bottom," Sydney said. "And before long, she'll be as fast as lightning!"

"Hmm." Kate shook her head as she looked at Sydney. "I doubt that. Have I mentioned that I'm no good at sports?"

"Only a thousand times. But don't think of this as a sport." Sydney's eyes lit with excitement. "I know! Think of yourself as one of those robots you and your dad like to build down in the basement at your house in Philly."

"Huh?" Kate gave her a curious look. "Me? A robot?"

"Sure." Sydney grew more animated by the minute. "If you had to build a robot that could ski—one that could get from the top of a hill to the bottom without falling down—how would you build him?"

"Well. . ." Kate demonstrated by putting her feet together and bending her knees. "He'd have to be really flexible. And he'd have to be able to shift to the right and the left to get the right momentum going, so his knees would have to bend. And he'd have to have a way to come to a quick stop, so I'd have to build him ankles that turned so he could stop in a hurry!"

"Exactly!" Sydney giggled. "You've got it! Just pretend *you're* that robot."

Kate laughed. "Okay. So what would you name me?"

"Hmm." Sydney paused, deep in thought. After a moment her eyes lit up. "I know! We'll call you Snow-Bot!"

"Snow-Bot it is!" Kate nodded. "So, show me what to do, O Sports Star, you!"

Sydney looked at her with a grin. "I can't believe I'm saying this, but let's hit the Rat!"

Kate looked down at the track winding alongside some trees. "Where does it lead?"

"Who cares?" Sydney called out. "That's half the fun. . . finding out! So, c'mon! Let's go!"

Just as they started to push off, a boy whizzed by them. He wore a red jacket and cap, but looked familiar. Kate watched as he soared down the hill, faster than anyone else.

"Oh, look Kate!" Sydney pointed with a worried look. "It's that boy. . .Michael."

"I wonder what he's doing here." Kate frowned. Hopefully he wasn't really going to enter the competition.

Sydney needed to win, after all!

"He's a great skier." Sydney watched him closely as he zipped down the hill, moving gracefully around every curve. "Doesn't look like he needs the practice." They watched him ski all the way from the top of the hill to the first curve, where they lost sight of him. At that point, Kate groaned.

"Wow." She didn't know what else to say. Michael *was* good.

"I'll bet he already has his Rat Pack T-shirt," Sydney said with a sigh. "He probably has a whole drawer full! Let's face it. . .I'll never win that competition on Saturday if he skis."

"Don't say that," Kate's mother said. "I'll bet you're just as fast!"

"Probably even faster," Kate added. "I don't know anyone who can run as fast as you. So surely you're just as fast on skis!"

"Only one way to know for sure." Sydney's expression brightened. "Let's go!"

She pushed off and led the way. Kate looked down, took a deep breath, said a little prayer, and then inched her way forward with her mother at her side.

To her surprise, she went slip-sliding down the tiny hill without falling. In fact, she went even faster than her mother, who tumbled into the snow at the first big curve.

Down, down, down Kate went. . .feeling almost like a bird taking flight. The cold wind blew against her cheeks, but she didn't mind. And though skiing was a little scary, Kate had to admit it was a lot more fun than she expected. *Maybe I really am a Snow-bot!*

On the other hand. . .she looked ahead. Sydney had almost made it to the bottom of the hill. Kate had almost caught up with her when something caught her attention. "Look out!"

Kate swerved to the right to avoid hitting a baby fawn. She tumbled head over heels, hollering the whole way. *Thump!* She ran straight into Sydney, who also took a tumble. Thankfully, Kate wasn't hurt. But when she looked up, Sydney was sitting in the snow, holding her ankle.

"Oh man!" Sydney's eyes glistened with tears.

"What is it?" Kate asked, drawing close.

Sydney groaned. "My ankle hurts. I guess I twisted it."

"How bad is it?" Kate knelt down in the snow, shivering from the cold. "Is it my fault? Did I hit you with my skis?"

"No, you didn't hit me. It's my own fault. I wasn't paying attention."

"Is it really bad?"

"I think I can walk on it." Sydney took a few steps, groaning the whole way. Each step looked more painful than the one before it.

"Do you think it's broken?" Kate asked. *Poor Sydney!*

"No. It's just twisted. I'm sure it'll be fine. When I get back to the inn, I'll put some ice on it and elevate it." After a few more steps, Sydney added, "Sure hope this doesn't keep me from being in the competition."

"We'll pray about that," Kate said. "The Lord knows you need that money for the mission trip. He's going to provide it one way or another."

Mrs. Oliver arrived. She took one look at Sydney and apologized. "I'm sorry we got separated! I made it down around the next curve before I realized you weren't with me. I took a little tumble, then came back up to look for you." She looked at the tears in Sydney's eyes and gasped. "Have you hurt yourself, honey?"

"A little," Sydney said. "My ankle hurts. I don't think it's very bad, but we should probably go back to the inn, just in case."

She hobbled beside Kate as they walked back to the car. Just as the girls reached the parking lot, Michael passed by. He gave them a funny look, but kept walking without speaking a word.

"Hey, there's Michael again." Kate watched as he disappeared into a crowd of people. *Something about that boy seems. . .weird.* Just as quickly, she was reminded not to judge him before knowing all the facts.

"He's really going to beat me now, especially if I'm injured." Sydney groaned.

"Don't talk like that!" Kate said. "You'll be fine. And you were almost to the bottom of the hill when I knocked you down. It's wasn't your fault."

"No, you don't understand. It was already hurting before

that. When I rounded the first turn, I think I twisted it!"

"When we get back to the inn, we'll elevate your ankle," Kate's mom said. "I'm sure it'll be fine in no time."

They drove back to the inn, where Aunt Molly greeted them with hot chocolate and peanut butter cookies, straight from the oven. She scolded Sydney, her gray curls bobbing up and down. "Sydney, you need to be careful! You could have hurt yourself out there."

"Oh, I'm fine." She forced a smile, but Kate could tell her friend was really in pain.

"Still, I've been skiing for years and I've never gotten hurt before." Sydney groaned. "It would have to happen the day I'm trying to teach Kate."

"I'm not a very good student." Kate shrugged. "I'm the reason she fell in the first place." She buried her face in her hands, trying to stop the tears. "I told you I was no good at sports!"

"Of course you are! You were doing a great job," Sydney said. "And I think you would have passed me, too!"

"You do?" Kate looked at her, stunned.

"I do." Sydney nodded. "So, don't be so hard on yourself!"

"You're a natural, Kate!" her mother added. "You need to stop saying you're no good at sports."

"Saying we're no good at sports is an Oliver family trait." Aunt Molly laughed. "Most of us in the Oliver family are more into technology." She turned to Kate. "Did you know your Uncle Ollie is working on a new mixer for the creamery? Michael's been helping him."

"Michael sure isn't helping him today," Sydney explained. "We just saw him skiing. He's really, really good."

"Ah." Aunt Molly nodded. "He's decided to enter the competition, then."

"I guess."

"Well, don't fret, Sydney. Let's just pray and see what God does. In the meantime, you girls scoot on out to the barn and take a plate of these cookies to your Uncle Ollie. They're his favorite."

"Maybe I can help him with his project," Kate said, growing excited. "I'd love to see all of the gadgets he's working on out there. Maybe I'll learn something new!"

Sydney laughed. "That sounds just like something you'd say, Kate. You're always more excited about learning than anything else."

"That's a special gift God has given her," Aunt Molly explained. "He's gifted her with. . ."

"Lots of brains?" Sydney asked.

Everyone laughed.

"Well, I *do* get a pretty big head sometimes," Kate said with a giggle, "especially when it comes to my science projects. But that doesn't mean I have more brains than anyone else."

"Still, you're the smartest girl in our club," Sydney said. "And I just know you'll figure out what's going on at the creamery. Before long this mystery will be solved."

"Yes, but who knows if the creamery will reopen." Aunt Molly sighed. "I talked to Geneva Hampton today, and she said the county health inspector is coming back for another inspection. Everyone is nervous they won't pass this time around."

"I still say there was something strange about that rat on the video," Kate said. "It looked different from other rats I've seen. I can't wait to hear back from McKenzie."

She thought about it as she trudged through the snow to get to the barn, where Uncle Ollie greeted her with a smile. Enough worrying about rats! For the rest of the day, she just wanted to do what she did best. . .work on gadgets and gizmos!

Hi-Ho, the Dairy-O

After the long day of skiing and helping Uncle Ollie in the barn, Kate finally fell asleep. Every muscle in her body ached from skiing, so she tossed and turned all night trying to get comfortable.

When she finally did fall into a deep sleep, Kate had a crazy dream. She was skiing through the Mad River Creamery, chasing rats! At the end of the dream, she fell into a humongous vat of curds and whey. For some reason, the woman in the white fur coat was swimming in there, too, with the mean man! And Michael was standing nearby with skis in his hand, talking about what a great competitor he was.

When she finally awoke, Kate found herself quoting the lines from "Little Miss Muffett." Totally strange!

She rubbed her eyes and looked at the clock. Seven thirty in the morning? Too early to be up, especially on a vacation.

She rolled over in the bed, wondering where Sydney was. Had she been swallowed by a giant rat, perhaps?

Kate rose from the bed, brushed her teeth, and dressed

in her warmest clothes. She had a feeling she knew just where Sydney would be. Sydney's foot had felt back to normal when they went to bed the night before. Minutes later—after shivering her way through several snowdrifts—Kate arrived in the barn and made her way back beyond Uncle Ollie's workshop to the small gym in the back. Uncle Ollie had added the gym, primarily for guests, a few years earlier. Sure enough, Sydney was on the treadmill. She looked at Kate and smiled, but never stopped walking.

"Hey, you're up early." Sydney dabbed at her forehead with a cloth.

"So are you." Kate yawned. "But you actually look like you're happy about it. I still want to be in bed!"

"I get up early every day now. Got to stay in shape, you know." Sydney stopped the elliptical machine and turned to face her. "Morning is the best time to exercise. It wakes up your body and gives you the energy to face the rest of the day. But the roads were icy this morning, so I decided this would be safer since my ankle is still a little weak. Uncle Ollie said it would be okay."

"He's probably just happy someone is actually using his workout room." Kate looked out of the window back toward the inn. In the early morning light, it looked even more beautiful, especially with snow stacked up in lovely white piles all around. "But can we talk about working out later? Aunt Molly is making oatmeal, and I never like to think about exercising and eating at the same time! Makes me nervous. Besides, I'd rather eat any day!"

"I suppose." Sydney shrugged, slowing her pace on the machine. "I can eat oatmeal. It's loaded with fiber and lots of vitamins. That's what I need to stay in shape for the competition. I just have to cut back on the brown sugar and butter, that's all."

Kate slapped herself in the forehead. "Good grief."

They trekked through the snow to the back door. As Kate swung it open, the wonderful aroma of cinnamon greeted them. "Yum!" Her tummy rumbled.

Minutes later they sat at the table. Kate warmed her hands against the steaming bowl of oatmeal. She breathed deeply, loving the smell of the cinnamon.

"I want to go back to the Rat today," Sydney said, taking a bite of her oatmeal.

Kate started to grumble, but then remembered how much she had enjoyed skiing. *Maybe I need to stop saying I'm no good at sports! I actually found one I like!* She took a bite of the oatmeal, smiling as she tasted the sugar, cinnamon, and butter. *Mmm. Aunt Molly knows just how I like it!*

Sydney fixed her own bowl, careful to add only the tiniest bit of brown sugar. Kate sighed as she watched her friend. Maybe if she tried—really, really tried—she could be athletic like Sydney.

Or not.

Thankfully, her little brother interrupted her thoughts. "I'm gonna build another snowman," Dexter said. "My other one fell over last night. Besides, he didn't look very good. He was kind of lumpy, and his nose fell off. I heard one of the kids in the neighborhood laughing at him. I think I'd better start over."

"You go right ahead and build a new one, honey," Aunt Molly said. "But remember to forgive those kids who made fun of you first!"

"I will." He nodded and skipped off to play outside.

Aunt Molly looked at Kate and winked. "You know what I always say. . . 'A snowman is the perfect man. He's very well rounded and comes with his own broom.'"

Kate laughed. "You're so funny, Aunt Molly."

"Why, thank you very much." Her aunt handed her a mug of hot cocoa.

"I want to go back to the creamery today," Kate said, then sipped the yummy cocoa.

"Go back?" Sydney gave her a funny look. "But it's closed down, right?"

"I don't mean go inside. I just want to look around outside. To. . ."

"Snoop?" Sydney asked. "Is that what you mean?" She paused for a moment then added, "I know what you're up to, Kate Oliver. You're determined, aren't you?"

"Well, maybe a little." Kate shrugged. "We'll only be in town till the end of the week, and I want to solve this case. If we spend all of our time practicing for the competition, we won't figure out who's sabotaging the creamery."

"Or *if* someone's sabotaging them," her aunt reminded her. "We still don't know."

"And we never will if Sydney and I don't get busy."

"True, true," Aunt Molly said.

Just then, Kate remembered something. "Before we leave, I need to check my e-mail to see if any of the other Camp Club Girls have written." She signed online and checked her e-mail.

The first was from McKenzie:

> *Been checking every species of rodent on the Web. Gross! The creature in the photo you sent has the body of a rat, but is a lot larger. It also has unusual fur. I can't find any other critters with fur like that! I will keep researching, I promise! In the meantime, keep me updated!*

The next e-mail was from Alexis:

> *Kate and Sydney, I have been researching the Mad River Valley Creamery. It's been in the area for over seventy years—owned by the Hampton family. The current owners—Luke and Geneva Hampton—inherited it from Luke's parents in 1986. Sales last year were higher than ever before. There is another*

*creamery called Cheese De-Lite in a town
about fifty miles away. Their sales aren't as
high as Mad River's, but they claim to have
the best cheese in the country. Cheese De-Lite
is owned by Mark and Abigail Collingsworth.
Their photos are on their company's Web site.*

Kate clicked the link and tried to go to the Web site
Alexis was talking about, but just then the Internet stopped
working. With a sigh, she rose from her seat. "I guess we
should really get over to the creamery anyway. We can go
skiing tomorrow, I promise."

The girls bundled up in their heavy coats and grabbed
scarves and mittens.

"It's extra-cold out today," Kate's mother said, "so don't
stay out long. Promise?"

"I promise, Mom." Kate kissed her mother on the cheek.
"Please pray for us, okay? I want to solve this case!"

"I will, honey. I'll pray that the Lord reveals every
hidden thing! Oh, and take Biscuit with you. I'll feel safer
knowing he's there. He's a great watchdog!"

"And a great crime solver!" Sydney added.

"Okay." Kate reached for Biscuit's leash. He jumped up
and down, excited to be going with them.

Minutes later, the girls headed on their way to the
creamery. Kate noticed how much colder it felt today.
"M–man!" she said with chattering teeth. "Maybe we

picked the wrong day for this!" She clung tight to Biscuit's leash and kept an eye on him.

"It's perfect ski weather." Sydney took a couple of steps, then slid a little. "Whoa." She paused to rub her ankle. "I've got to be more careful on this weak ankle! I almost fell."

"Better watch out! We've got to get that ankle healed by Saturday, so no more falling!" Kate said.

When they arrived at the creamery, they found it closed, just as Kate suspected. There were no cars out front—not even the Hamptons' SUV.

"So sad," she said, shaking her head.

"Now what do we do?" Sydney pulled her scarf tighter and looked at Kate. "How can we snoop if the place is closed down?"

"Let's go around back. We've never seen the back of the building before."

"You're not thinking of sneaking inside, are you?" Sydney asked. "'Cause if you are. . ."

"No, no. I wouldn't do that. I'm just looking to see. . ." Kate shrugged. "I don't know. Something. Anything."

Biscuit tugged on the leash, leading them to the back of the creamery. Once there, they looked at anything and everything—the doors, windows, even the alleyway behind the back parking lot. All the while, Biscuit kept his nose to the ground sniffing, sniffing, sniffing. Kate wondered what he might be smelling. *Probably all of that cheese!*

"This place is huge!" Sydney said. "I had no idea it went back this far."

"It *is* big. And it's different from any building I've ever seen before." Kate pointed. "Oh, look. There's the Dumpster."

"So?" Sydney gave her a funny look. "You're not going to make me climb in and look for evidence, are you?"

"No." Kate laughed. "But it would make a funny picture to send the other girls. I'm just looking to see evidence of rodents."

"Rodents. . .gross!" Sydney shuddered. "You think they've been hiding out in the Dumpster?"

"If they're looking for leftovers!" Kate giggled.

"Dis–*gus*–ting!" Sydney said, then laughed.

They looked all around the Dumpster, but saw nothing suspicious. Kate even checked the edges of the building, finally noticing some footprints in the snow. "Oh, Sydney, check this out. These look like tennis shoe prints."

"So?" Sydney shrugged. "Mr. Hampton probably wears tennis shoes."

"No, he wears hiking boots. I remember looking the other day. These prints start at the edge of the parking lot and go all the way to the back door." Kate pulled on the door handle, but it didn't open. "Hmm. Locked." Biscuit began to whimper and pawed at the door. "Looks like he wants in there, too."

"He's a cheese-a-holic!" Sydney said. "He wants inside so he can eat all of the cheese!"

Kate laughed and said, "Probably," then pulled Biscuit

away from the building.

"Lots of people probably use that door," Sydney said, rubbing her hands together.

"I don't think so." Kate shook her head, deep in thought. This looked like the kind of door that rarely got used. "Maybe someone snuck in through this door to put rats inside."

"If so, wouldn't we see evidence of the rats? Maybe. . . droppings." Sydney looked like she might be sick as she said the word.

"Ooo, so true!" Kate dropped to her knees and looked around. After a few minutes she rose back up again and shrugged. "Don't see anything."

Pulling out her camera, she began to take pictures of the footprints. "At least we have this evidence."

"Little good it does us," Sydney said. "Just footprints in the snow. Big deal."

"But it might be a big deal," Kate reminded her. "You never know."

She snapped several photographs as she followed the trail of footprints back to the edge of the parking lot. "They disappear right here." She sighed. "Oh well."

An idea came to her. "If we measure the footprints, we should be able to determine the shoe size."

"How will that help?" Sydney asked, wrinkling her nose in confusion.

"It will help us eliminate suspects," Kate explained.

"Are you saying you have a measuring tape with you?" Sydney looked at her as if she didn't believe such a thing was possible.

"I do! It's a digital measuring tape and it records the measurements. I can't believe I haven't shown it to you before." She pulled it out of her pocket and measured the prints. "Hmm. It's 10.31 inches. I wonder what size that is."

"Well, it's not as big as your dad's shoes," Sydney observed. "But it's lots bigger than Dexter's." She stuck her foot in the footprint and shrugged. "Bigger than mine, too, and I've got pretty big feet!"

"I'm guessing it's a size eight or nine in a men's shoe," Kate said, putting the digital measuring tape away. "But we can ask my dad later."

Her cell phone rang, startling her. Kate looked at the number and smiled when she saw it was her dad. "Hi, Dad! Wow, that's a crazy coincidence! I was just talking about you."

"You were?" He laughed. "Good things, I hope."

"I need your help. We've measured some footprints. They're 10.31 inches long. What size man's shoe would that be?"

"Hmm. I might have to look that one up on the Internet," he said. "Or, measure my own feet! But before I do that, let me tell you why I'm calling. We've decided to go to the restaurant in town for lunch. Want me to swing by and pick you girls up?"

"Oh, we can walk," Kate said, her teeth chattering.

"No, honey. The temperature has really dropped. Your mother is worried you and Sydney will get frostbite. We're coming by that way, so meet us out front. Besides, we'll need to drop Biscuit back off at the inn before going to the restaurant. Oh, and Kate. . ."

"Yes, Dad?"

"How's the investigation going?"

She sighed. "Other than a few footprints, we haven't found anything suspicious. This case might just turn out to be a dead end. Maybe the creamery isn't being sabotaged, after all."

"Well, don't sound so depressed about that!" He laughed. "We want a happily-ever-after ending to this Christmas vacation, don't we?"

"Sure. But if there's really no case to solve, then I've wasted a lot of hours on our family vacation when I should have been hanging out with my family. And I've spent way too much time outdoors when I could have been sitting next to the fireplace drinking Aunt Molly's hot cocoa."

"Aw, honey, your mother and I know how much you girls love to investigate. So you go right ahead and do what comes naturally."

"Are you calling me a natural-born snoop?" Kate asked.

"If the shoe fits. . ." He laughed again. "But I am a little concerned about how much time you kids have been spending outdoors in this weather. I don't want you catching cold. . .especially right before Christmas!"

"Yes, and poor Biscuit is shivering," Kate said. "I feel bad for him. We should buy him a sweater!"

"We'll do that," her dad said. "In the meantime, we'll be by to pick you girls up in about ten minutes."

"Okay, Dad. Oh, and Dad?"

"Yes, honey?"

"I love you. Thanks so much for understanding."

"Love you, too, kiddo."

As they ended the call, something caught Kate's attention. A car pulled around the back of the creamery through the alley. She and Sydney slipped behind a Dumpster and watched. Kate did her best to keep Biscuit quiet, but he kept whimpering. "Hush, boy!" she whispered.

"Wow, that's a great car. A Jaguar!" Sydney whispered, her eyes wide with excitement. "Do you suppose the Hamptons own a car that fancy?"

Kate shook her head. "They don't seem the type. Besides, I saw Mr. Hampton drive away in an SUV the other day, not a Jaguar."

"Seems kind of weird that a fancy car like that would be in an alley behind a creamery," Sydney said. She peeked out once again, then pulled her head back with a worried look on her face. "We'd better be careful. I think they're slowing down."

The tires crunched against the icy pavement, finally stopping. A woman stepped out and looked around in every direction, then signaled and a man got out. Biscuit began to growl. Kate pulled on his leash to get him to stop, but he refused.

Kate gasped. "Do you see who that is?" she whispered. "It's the woman who fainted the other day. . .and her husband."

"Oh yeah." Sydney squinted. "The woman in the expensive coat and the man with the sour look on his face." Sydney paused a moment to look at them. "Ooo! He looked this way. I hope he didn't see us."

They watched as the man and woman walked across the back of the building. He seemed to be looking for something. At one point, he stood on his toes and tried to look into a window. Biscuit yipped, but Kate tapped him on the nose and whispered, "Shush!"

"Why do you suppose that man is looking inside?" Kate whispered to Sydney. "He just went on the tour the other day, so he knows what the building looks like on the inside."

"I don't know," Sydney said. "But it's really suspicious. Oh!" She paused, then looked at Kate with a gleam in her eye. "Kate, look! He's wearing tennis shoes!"

Kate squinted to see the man's white tennis shoes.

"Wow!" she whispered. "You're right."

That didn't necessarily make him a suspect, but it did make her wonder!

They continued to watch the man. He put his hand on the doorknob of the back door and tried it, but it wouldn't turn. Once again, Biscuit started to growl. Kate tried to quiet him. "He's trying to break in!" she whispered.

"We don't know that for sure," Sydney said. "After all, we tried that knob, too, and we weren't trying to break in."

"True." Kate shook her head as she watched the man. He walked to another window and looked inside, then continued across the icy parking lot to the side of the building.

"It's like he's looking over every detail of the building," Sydney whispered. "Like he's scoping it out. But, why?"

"I wish I knew! Something is odd about him, for sure," Kate said.

"Do you think they have something to do with the rats?" Sydney asked. "Maybe we should find out who these people are and see if there's any connection."

Just then Kate's cell phone rang. . .loudly! Then Biscuit started barking even more loudly!

"Oh no!" she whispered. She reached to silence the phone, but the man turned and looked in their direction. "Hush, Biscuit! Hush!" Kate pressed the IGNORE button on her phone and took a couple of deep breaths. "Look the other way. Look the other way," she whispered as she watched the man.

However, instead of looking the other way. . .he began to walk right toward them! Kate's heart felt like it might explode.

"Lord, help us!" she whispered. "Please!"

CHAPTER 8

The Plot Thickens

Kate's heart raced as the stranger's shoes crunched through the snow in their direction. *Oh no! Please turn around!*

"What is it, Mark?" the woman called out. "What are you doing over there?"

"I heard something behind the Dumpster," he hollered back. "I'm checking it out."

Kate squatted and tried to hide on the farthest side of the Dumpster, praying he wouldn't see them. Unfortunately, the closer he came, the more Biscuit growled.

Just when Kate was sure they would be discovered, a car horn beeped from the front of the creamery.

"It's Dad!" Kate mouthed to Sydney.

The woman hollered out, "Mark! C'mon, let's get out of here before we get caught!"

"I'm out of here!" The man ran back toward his car, and the woman joined him. Seconds later, they went speeding off.

The car disappeared back into the alleyway and Biscuit ran after it, barking at the top of his lungs. Kate sat shivering behind the Dumpster. "I c–can't b–believe they didn't c–catch us."

"I know! That scared me *so* bad!" Sydney said, her eyes wide with fear. "I've never been that scared!"

"Me either! What do you think they were doing here?" Kate asked. "Do you think they put the rats in the store the other day? Seems pretty obvious, if they did!"

"I don't know, but it sure is suspicious!" Sydney said. She glanced Kate's way, still looking nervous. "Oh, by the way, who called?"

Kate glanced at the caller ID on the phone. "Bailey. I'll call her back later. No time to talk right now!"

"Just wait till she hears what she interrupted!" Sydney said.

The girls heard a horn honk again.

"That's my dad," Kate said. "He's probably getting worried. Let's make a run for it!"

Sydney took off running and Kate followed. As always, she could barely keep up with her friend. "I've. . .been. . . eating. . .too. . .much. . .cheese!" she said as she slid back and forth across the slippery pavement. "It's. . .slowing. . . me. . .down!"

"Just. . .keep. . .going!" Sydney called out. "You'll make it!"

As they rounded the front of the building, the girls saw the Olivers' car. Kate was never so happy to see her parents. She opened the car door and climbed in, happy to find it warm inside. Biscuit jumped in on top of her, his wet paws making her colder than ever. "Sit, boy!"

He curled up next to her on the seat, panting.

"I th—thought I w—was going to f—freeze out there!" she said with chattering teeth. Her hands were shaking so hard, she could barely close the door.

"So, any more suspicious stuff to report?" Dexter asked, looking up from his handheld video game.

"Is there ever!" Kate told the whole story about the man and the woman.

Her mother gave her a stern look.

"Kate Oliver, this is getting dangerous. You're in over your head. I think it's time to call the police."

"I understand your concerns." Kate's father reached over to pat her hand. "But let's not get too worked up. It was just a car in a parking lot. No one set off any alarms or anything. And the girls are fine." He looked at them both. "You are fine, aren't you?"

Kate nodded and Sydney muttered a quick, "Uh-huh." However, inside, Kate still felt like a bowl full of jelly! She quivered all over! Was it from the cold. . .or fear?

"We'd better get Biscuit back to the inn," Kate's mother said. "He looks tired."

Minutes later, they dropped him off at the inn. The adults chatted all the way to the restaurant, but Kate couldn't seem to say a word. Instead, she just kept thinking about the man. Why was he scoping out the building? Were the footprints his? He was wearing tennis shoes, after all.

They arrived at the restaurant in just a few minutes. As they started to get out of the car, Kate's father turned her way.

"Before we go inside, give me your digital measuring tape and I'll measure my feet," he said.

"Why in the world would you do that?" Kate's mother asked. "And in a restaurant parking lot, of all places!"

"I'm trying to help Kate solve a big case!" He pulled off his shoes and Kate handed him the measuring tape. After a moment, he said, "My feet are 10.7 inches long and I wear a size ten. So I'm going to guess your suspect is probably a size nine in a men's shoe."

"What makes you think it's a man?" Aunt Molly asked. "Maybe that woman with the white coat has extra-large feet!"

"Good point." Kate shrugged. "We really don't know." As they walked into the restaurant, she leaned over and whispered to Sydney, "Hey, what size feet do you think that man had? The one behind the creamery, I mean."

"I wasn't looking at his feet, Kate," Sydney said, shaking her head. "Honestly! I was too busy trying not to get caught!"

"Yeah, me, too." Kate sighed, then whispered a prayer of thanks. *Thank You, Lord, that we didn't get hurt back there. Thanks for sending my dad at just the right moment!*

As they entered the restaurant, Kate's wrist began to buzz. "Oh! I have an e-mail on my Internet wristwatch." As they waited to be seated, she checked it.

"Who was it?" Sydney asked.

"Elizabeth. She just wanted to let us know she was praying for us this morning."

"Wow!" Sydney smiled. "I'm glad she was! What a cool

coincidence! We really needed it, didn't we? Her timing was perfect!"

"It sure was!" Kate agreed.

"That's how God works," Aunt Molly said with a nod. "He works out every detail in His perfect timing."

The hostess led the Oliver family to a booth, and everyone sat down. As soon as she got the menu, Kate began to look over it. Her stomach was rumbling, and she could hardly wait to eat!

Just then she heard a familiar voice. Looking up, she saw Michael in the next booth, talking to the waitress.

"Hi, Michael," Kate called out. She waved, trying to be friendly.

He looked her way and nodded, then turned back to his handheld video game, not even pretending to be nice.

"Humph." Kate crossed her arms at her chest.

"Be quick to forgive, honey," Aunt Molly reminded her. "Even when others don't respond the way they should. That's the perfect time to forgive. . .before you get upset."

"Yes, but he *never* responds the way he should," Sydney said quietly. "And have you noticed he never looks happy?"

"And why is he sitting all alone in a restaurant?" Kate asked. "That's weird."

"Oh, I can explain that part. His mother is a waitress here." Aunt Molly pointed at a woman with dark hair pulled back in a ponytail. "That's who he was talking to. Her name is Maggie. She's worked here for as long as I can remember, so Michael spends a lot of his free time here. Keeps him from being lonely, I guess."

"I see." Kate raised her menu, trying to hide the fact that she was snooping.

"The poor kid's been through a lot," Uncle Ollie said with a sad look on his face. "His dad left when he was only three, and now, of course, Michael has lost his grandpa. So anything we can do to keep him from being too lonely is a good thing."

"Oh, I know, but there's something about him that worries me." Sydney shook her head. "I don't know what it is, exactly. Just. . .something."

"Are you worried he'll beat you in the contest?" Uncle Ollie asked with a mischievous twinkle in his eye. " 'Cause I have it on good authority you're pretty fast. I wouldn't worry if I were you."

"Oh, I'm not worried. I promise."

Kate looked at her friend, wishing she could read her thoughts.

Uncle Ollie rose from his seat and invited Michael to join them at their table. He came, but he didn't look happy. When he sat next to Kate, she tried to smile. . .tried to be friendly. But he didn't make it easy! He sat there like a bump on a log, just staring at his Nintendo DS Lite while everyone else talked.

Kate's cell phone rang, and she looked at the number. "Oh, it's Bailey! I forgot to call her back." She looked at her mother and asked, "Can I answer it? Do you mind?"

"Go ahead, honey," her mom said. "Just don't be long. We need to order our food soon."

Kate nodded, then answered the phone with a smile. "Hey, Bailey! What's up?"

"I found some information online," Bailey said, sounding breathless and overly excited, as always. "Did you know the Mad River Creamery fired their security guard several months ago?"

"No. How did you find that out?"

"I googled the name *Mad River Creamery* and went to every site that came up. Every one. Way down on the list I found a blogsite that belongs to some nameless person, complaining about someone being fired from the creamery this past summer."

"Really? But you don't know who owns that blog? That's weird."

"Really weird!" Bailey said. "It was all very suspicious. Just sort of a warning for readers to stay away from the creamery. I guess this person was the one who got fired. Or maybe a relative or a friend. . .something like that."

"Ooo, the plot thickens!" Kate looked at Sydney in anticipation and whispered, "There's more to this than meets the eye!"

Sydney looked surprised, but didn't say anything. Instead, she stared at Michael out of the corner of her eye, as if she didn't trust him.

"Did the Web site mention anything about rats?" Kate asked Bailey.

As she said the word *rats*, everyone at the table looked her way. Kate's mother shook her head, as if to say, "This is not appropriate dinner table conversation, Kate!" Kate mouthed the words "I'm sorry," then put her hand over her mouth, waiting for Bailey's response.

After a moment, Bailey said, "No, but there was plenty of stuff on there about getting even!"

"Very suspicious. Makes me wonder. . ." Kate started to say more, but noticed the look on her mom's face. "Bailey, can I call you back later? We're in a restaurant right now, and I need to order my meal."

"Sure. I'll text you if I find out anything else."

"Please do."

Kate ended the call and turned back to everyone at the table with a cheery voice. "So, what's everyone going to order? I'm starved!" She opened the menu and pointed to a large baked potato with all of the trimmings. "Mmm! This looks good. I'm going to get this." After a moment, her gaze shifted to a picture of roast beef with mashed potatoes and gravy. "Or this! Yummy! I haven't had roast and potatoes in ages. And can we order dessert after, Mom? I'm starved!"

She pointed to a picture of coconut cream pie. "They have my favorite!"

"I like the cherry pie," Dexter said, pointing at another picture.

"Their apple pie is great," Uncle Ollie added, "but not as great as your Aunt Molly's!"

"Pie has a lot of empty calories, Kate," Sydney whispered. "It's not really good for you."

"Empty?" Kate looked at her friend, curious.

"That just means it's not really good for you, but it's fattening," Sydney explained. "Most sweets are nothing but empty calories."

"Oh." Kate closed the menu and thought about that for a minute. Finally, she cheered up. "But I feel full after I eat pie, not empty. So it can't be all bad, right?" She flashed a smile at Sydney, who laughed.

"I love you, Kate," Sydney said. "You always see the good in everything."

"Especially in food!" Kate giggled. "And I'm starving right now!"

"Solving mysteries makes you hungry, eh?" her father asked. "That's my girl. But you'll never *really* starve, that's for sure!"

"Nope! I have the best appetite in town."

"And the best nose for snooping," her mother added. "And I'm assuming Bailey was calling with news about the creamery?"

"Well, yes, but. . ." She shrugged. "I don't want to bother you guys with this while we're eating."

"Tell us," Aunt Molly said. "We want to know."

"Well, Bailey thinks maybe she's stumbled across a clue.

Something that will help us figure out who's sabotaging the creamery."

"*If* someone's sabotaging the creamery," Aunt Molly reminded her. "We still don't know for sure."

"Yes." Kate nodded. "That's true." Even as she spoke the words, however, she knew that it *was* true. Someone was trying to sabotage the creamery. And she would figure out who. . .and why!

"What's the deal with you girls?" Michael rolled his eyes. "Why is it so important to figure this out? What are you trying to prove, anyway?"

"Trying to prove?" Kate asked, confused. "Nothing, really."

"We just like to help people." Sydney shrugged. "It's what we do."

"And they're good at it!" Dexter added.

Michael rolled his eyes. "Why do you want to help those Hamptons?" He muttered something under his breath.

"Don't you like the Hamptons?" she asked.

Instead of answering, he got up and left the restaurant without even saying good-bye.

"Well, that was strange," Aunt Molly said with a stunned expression.

"Very!" Kate's mother added.

"Not like him at all," Ollie added. "In fact, I've never seen this side of him. Very odd."

"I'm telling you, something about that boy bothers me,"

Sydney added. "I can't put my finger on it, but he's just. . . weird." After a second, she looked ashamed. "I'm sorry. I shouldn't have said that. I'm trying not to judge people, and look what I just did." She sighed.

"We all make mistakes," Kate added, "but you're right about the fact that something about him seems suspicious."

Thankfully, the waitress showed up at the table.

"Hi, Maggie!" Aunt Molly said with a smile. "Good to see you."

"Well, it's great to see you, too," she said. "You're my favorite customers, you know."

"She says that to all of her customers," Uncle Ollie whispered in Kate's ear.

"I heard that, Ollie Oliver, and you know it's not true!" Maggie grinned. "You folks are my very favorite." She looked around and asked, "Hey, what happened to that son of mine? I thought I saw him sitting here with you."

"He was." Uncle Ollie shook his head. "Not sure what happened, but he left in a hurry."

"Hmm." She shook her head. "He's been acting mighty strange since my pop. . ." Maggie's eyes filled with tears, and Kate suddenly felt very sorry for her.

"I'm sorry," Kate said, feeling a lump grow in her throat. How terrible it must be to lose your father! She looked over at her dad and tried—just for a moment—to imagine it. The idea was so painful she pushed it away immediately.

"Sorry to get all emotional on you." Maggie wiped the tears out of her eyes with the back of her hand and smiled. "What would you like to order, folks?"

Kate ordered the soup and sandwich combo, then listened as everyone else ordered. Everything sounded so good! At the end, she changed her order to a burger and fries to match her dad's.

While they waited for the food, Sydney changed the topic to the upcoming competition.

"Do you think you're ready, honey?" Aunt Molly asked.

"I don't know. I've only had one practice," Sydney said. "But Kate and I are going back to the Rat tomorrow so I can try again."

"I'm glad you're learning to ski, Kate," Aunt Molly said. "And you never know. . .we may turn you into a sports fan after all!"

"That would be the day!" Kate's father said. "My girl is far too busy helping me with all of my gadgets and gizmos to think about sports when we're home. That's one reason I'm glad we're in Mad River Valley. She can stop thinking about electronics and start thinking about just being a kid!"

Kate shrugged. "Skiing is okay, but you know me, Dad. I'd rather be working on one of the robots with you."

After a moment's pause, she added, "Oh, and by the way. . .speaking of robots. . ." She went on to tell him Sydney's idea about the snow-bot.

"Snow-bot?" He looked at her with a sparkle in his eyes. "What a marvelous idea. Maybe when we get home, we could actually build a little snow-bot and use it for ski demonstrations! Can't you see it now?" He went off on a tangent, talking about how they could sell the robot to people who wanted to learn how to ski.

"Wonderful idea!" Uncle Ollie threw in.

"Hey, it was my idea," Sydney said with a pretend pout. "If you make millions off of this robot, do I get some of the profits?"

"Of course, of course!" Kate's dad laughed. "You'll get a percentage and so will Kate. Who knows. . ." He grinned from ear to ear. "Snow-bot might just be a big hit!"

"Oh, I hope so!"

Everyone went on to talk about skiing, but Kate's thoughts were on something else. She kept thinking about what happened at the creamery. The man and woman in the car. . .what were they doing there? Something about them just didn't seem right. And what was up with those footprints? Did they belong to the man. . .or someone else? How would she ever find out?

Glancing out of the window, she happened to notice Michael passing by. The minute she saw him, a chill came over her. Something about him made her very nervous. Very nervous, indeed.

With a sigh, she turned back to her family and friends,

determined to stay focused on the important things. *Lord, don't ever let me forget the people who are right in front of me! They're more important than any case!*

Right now, the investigation could wait!

CHAPTER 9

Lost in the Maze

On Friday, just one day before the big competition, Kate went with Sydney to ski one more time. This time she wasn't as nervous as before. In fact, she almost looked forward to it.

"I'm getting faster every time!" Sydney said, looking more confident than she had in days. "But there are still a couple of areas that slow me down. I need to figure out how to pick up speed in those places!"

"Yes, there are some crazy twists and turns on the course," Kate agreed. After all, she'd already fallen several times and had the bruises to prove it!

"I think I can make it to the bottom without falling this time," Sydney said. "But I want to increase my speed in the tricky places. So let's do our best to get to the bottom in record time today, okay?"

"Sure. And I'll time us." Kate pointed to her super-duper wristwatch. "I'll bet you're the fastest one out there!"

"Hardly!" Sydney laughed. "But maybe I'll do better today than last time."

The girls dressed in their warmest clothes and prepared to head off to the slopes.

"Do you think you'll be okay without me?" Kate's mom asked. "Molly and I have plans to visit Michael's mother today. She seems a little lonely, so we want to cheer her up by taking her to the tearoom for some girl time."

"That's sweet, Mom," Kate said. "But don't worry about us. Mad River Valley is a safe place. Nothing'll happen."

"They'll be fine," Aunt Molly assured her. "It's a safe course, and lots of people are around. Don't fret!"

"Well, just stay as warm as you can." Kate's mom handed her some money. "And if you get cold, go inside and buy some hot chocolate. Promise? And don't forget to call if you need anything. We're just a few minutes away."

"I promise, Mom." Kate grinned. "But don't worry! I'm twelve now, remember? And it's not like I haven't been to the slopes before. We just went the other day. This time I'm sure it will be even easier than before."

"I know, but it's hard to watch your children grow up and do things on their own!" Kate's mom shrugged and her eyes misted.

Kate gave her a hug and whispered, "I promise not to grow up *too* fast." She wondered what it would feel like to be a mom, watching your child do something alone for the first time.

A few minutes later, Uncle Ollie drove Kate and Sydney to the ski area. As he stopped the car, he gave them a warning. "We're expecting more snow this afternoon, girls, so finish skiing early. I'll be here to pick you up at two o'clock. I think that will give you plenty of time. Try to be here waiting so I don't have to come looking for you."

"We'll be here!" Kate said. She waved good-bye as she and Sydney headed across the parking lot with their skis.

When they arrived at the ski lift, this time Kate wasn't as scared to get on it. In fact, she looked forward to it. As they rode up, up, up the hill, she breathed in the fresh morning air and hollered, "I love it here!" to Sydney, who was in the seat below hers. Her voice echoed against the snow-packed mountain. *This place doesn't just look awesome; it sounds awesome!* she thought.

Finally, they reached the top of the slope. Even though Kate wanted to ski, she still felt a little nervous. She and Sydney made their way to the Rat, and Sydney looked at her with a grin. "I'm overcoming my fear of rats by skiing here!"

"Me, too!" Kate giggled. "Funny, huh? Think of all the stories we'll have to tell the other girls!"

Kate rubbed her gloved hands together for warmth before reaching for her poles. Then she and Sydney took off soaring down the hill. The crisp, cold wind whipped at her face, making it tingle. In fact, it was so cold that her arms and legs began to ache.

The first big turn caught Kate off guard, and she almost fell. Thankfully, she got control of herself and made it without tumbling. A short time later, she came to a small drop-off.

"Woo!" she hollered as she soared into the air, then landed gracefully below. *I can't believe I did that!*

Now for the hard part. The next part of the course was filled with twists and turns, and there were some trees ahead. *Better steer clear of those, for sure!*

She bent her knees and leaned into the course, picking up speed as she rounded the first sharp turn. Then the second. As she came to the section of trees, she leaned to the left to avoid them.

Just as Kate sailed into a clearing, she heard a terrible cry. To her left, Sydney tumbled head over heels into the snow.

"Oh no!" Kate got so distracted watching her friend that she lost her footing and tipped over sideways. She landed on her bottom in the snow. It didn't hurt too badly, but then she rolled a couple of times and banged her elbow into a rock. "Ouch!"

Finally coming to a stop, she pulled off her skis and ran to Sydney's side. "Are you okay? What's happened?"

Sydney sat in the snow, gripping her ankle with tears streaming down her face. "Oh, Kate. It's my ankle! It's worse! *Much* worse. I think I've really hurt it this time!"

"What did you do?"

"I don't know. It was already hurting this morning when I walked on the treadmill. I guess I should have told someone, but I didn't. I thought I could make it stronger by walking on it, but I guess I was wrong."

"Oh, Sydney!"

"I feel like I've twisted it again. But it hurts so bad! Much worse than before."

"What should we do?" Kate asked, looking around. Oh, if only someone else would come by and offer to help! What made her think they could come to the slopes alone?

"I. . .I think we need to go back," Sydney stammered. "Do you mind?"

"Of course not!" Kate looked around again, hoping for some help. The mountainside remained empty. The only thing she heard was the sound of her voice echoing against the snow. "Will we have to walk down to the bottom?"

"I guess." Sydney looked around. "But I don't think I'll make it, to be honest. Maybe there's a trail closer to the trees. It's too dangerous to be out in the open like this. Any moment a skier could come flying down the hill and run us over!"

"Oh, I never thought of that!" Kate held tight to her limping friend's arm and led her to some trees.

When they got there, Sydney gripped her ankle and began to cry harder. "I can't believe I did this! I'm never going to get to go on my mission trip now."

"Don't worry about that right now," Kate said. "One thing at a time."

She looked around, a little confused about where they were. Just then a bit of falling snow caught her attention. "Oh no! It's snowing again. Uncle Ollie said it wasn't supposed to snow till this afternoon."

"That's not good, Kate. We can't get stuck out here in the snow, especially if my ankle is too weak to go to the bottom of the hill!"

"I know, but what can we do?" Kate started to tremble.

"We've got to get back to the parking lot somehow." Sydney dabbed at her eyes with gloved hands. "Do you think you can help me?"

"I'll try." Kate looked around. "But which way is the parking lot? I'm confused."

"I think it's east?" Sydney looked up with pain in her eyes. "Do you have a compass?"

"Yes." Kate pulled out her digital measuring tape with the built-in compass. "Okay, east is this way." She pointed to their left. "You're sure it's east, right?"

"I think so." Sydney shrugged. "But right now I'm in so much pain, I'm not sure about anything."

A cold wind blew over them, making an eerie sound against the backdrop of the mountain. Kate shivered.

"Wow. That was creepy. Sounded like the mountain was crying."

"No, I'm the only one crying," Sydney said, forcing a smile.

"Would it be better if I went after someone to help carry you back?" Kate offered. She hated to leave Sydney here, but she didn't know what else to do.

"No, I think I can hop on my good foot, as long as we go slow. Just help me, Kate. Please." Sydney rose to her feet, almost falling over. She leaned against Kate.

"Take slow, steady steps," Kate said. "And let me do most of the work."

She had never seen Sydney like this before. Usually Sydney was the one running races or playing sports. But now—with an injured ankle—would she even be able to ski in the competition? It was only a couple of days away. What would happen if she didn't win the three hundred dollars? Would she get to go on the mission trip?

After the girls had been walking a few minutes, the snow began to fall even harder.

"It–it's blinding me," Kate said, shivering. "I can't see more than a few feet."

"And I'm getting colder by the minute," Sydney added. "It's making my ankle hurt worse."

They followed what looked like a trail. It wound in and out, in and out, and seemed to lead absolutely nowhere. They faced dead ends at every turn!

"Now I know what a mouse feels like, hunting for cheese in a maze," Kate said, then groaned. "No wonder they call this slope the Rat. It just like being trapped inside a gigantic trap!"

Minutes later, Sydney shook her head. "I have to stop for a minute, Kate. It hurts too much to keep going. Stop. Please."

"Of course." Kate stopped, grateful to find a spot under some trees where the snow was packed tight. After watching Sydney rub her ankle, Kate had an idea. "Oh, I can't believe I didn't think of this sooner!"

"What?"

"I have a GPS tracker on my cell phone. I can type in the name of the lodge next to the parking lot, and the tracker will lead us back. . .no problem."

The wind began to howl louder and louder, and the girls huddled together. Off in the distance, the skies began to look heavy and gray.

Kate opened her phone and waited for a signal. "Come on." She shook the phone, frustrated. "Work! Please work!" A few seconds later, she had a faint signal. Kate quickly typed in the name of the lodge.

"Pray, Sydney," she said. "This has to work."

"Okay. I'm praying." Sydney's eyes were filled with tears, and Kate knew her ankle must really be hurting. Sydney never complained!

A couple of minutes later, just as Kate started to get her hopes up, she lost the signal on her phone. She closed it with a sigh. "What's the point of having GPS tracking if I can't get a signal?"

A burst of cold air caught her by surprise, and she began to shake. "Is it getting colder, or am I just imagining it?"

"I—it's g—getting c—colder. And the snow is really coming down now. See?" Sydney pointed to the skies, then huddled next to Kate, shaking. She closed her eyes. "I don't know why, but I'm suddenly getting tired."

"It's the altitude. And the dark skies."

Kate looked up. The sky hung heavy over them, a sure sign that a heavy snowfall was on its way.

"W—what are we going to do?" Sydney broke down in tears.

Kate had never seen this side of Sydney before. Usually her friend was the strong one. . .the brave one.

Now I have to be strong and brave!

"They're going to find us," Kate said, doing her best to sound confident. "We've got the transmitters on our snow boots, remember? That's the very best tracking device."

"Yes, but your Uncle Ollie's not coming back till two o'clock," Sydney reminded her. "It will be hours before they even realize we're missing. No one will know to look for a signal till then, and I'll be frozen stiff by two o'clock!"

"Don't say that!" Just the thought of it sent a shiver down Kate's spine.

"I'm sorry." Sydney pulled at the scarf around her neck. "I don't know why I'm so scared."

"It's normal when things go wrong. Just keep praying, Sydney."

"I need to," her friend said. "My throat is starting to feel funny. And my eyes sting from the ice."

"Would you be okay for a minute if I went to look for someone to help?" Kate asked. "I'll come right back, I promise."

Sydney leaned against the tree and nodded. "Just

promise you won't stay gone long. And leave a trail so you know how to get back to me. I don't want to get stuck out here alone."

"Me either. I'll follow my footprints back." As soon as Kate spoke the word *footprints*, she remembered the footprints they'd found behind the creamery. Would they ever figure out who was sabotaging the Hamptons?

This isn't the time to worry about that!

Kate hated to leave her friend, but she wanted to check something. If she was remembering correctly, there was an old red barn just south of here. She'd seen it yesterday when the skies were clear. If they could just make it to that barn, they could warm up. And maybe she could get better reception there, too. If so, she could call her father or Uncle Ollie on her cell phone. They would come in a hurry!

A few minutes later, Kate found a trail. It wound through tangles of brush and snowcapped trees. She turned to the right and then the left, trying to get her bearings. *Lord, help me. Please.* A tree branch slapped her in the face, and snow flew everywhere.

"Oh!" The pain shot through her cheek, and she ducked to wedge her way underneath the low snow-covered branches.

A few seconds later, she heard the strangest sound. . . like something falling and hitting the earth below. Taking a step, she heard a *c-ra-ack!* The ground underneath her shifted, and she started to tumble forward!

Down, down, down she went. . .praying all the way!

Along Came a Spider

Kate tumbled down through several layers of snow and ice until she landed with a *thud* on an icy patch of ground. She rubbed at her backside and cried out in pain. "Oh, help!" Right away, she began to pray. "Lord, get me out of here. Please!"

Pushing her weight backward, she landed on sturdy ground. However, the place where she stood just seconds before collapsed. Down, down, down it went, making a crashing sound below.

She peeked over the edge, realizing she'd almost stepped off the edge of a drop-off. Somehow she had stopped. . .just in time! Kate's heart thumped hard against her chest. How close she'd come to falling! Another look convinced her it was a long way to the bottom. *I could have died!* Something—or *Someone*—had saved her, just in the nick of time!

And where was the crackling sound coming from? She still heard it off in the distance. Squinting against the blinding snow, she saw something that looked like a frozen waterfall to her right. Pieces of the ice had broken off and fallen into the spot way down below. The frozen water led down to the place where she might have landed, if she'd taken one more step.

Whoa! Talk about a long drop! Thank You, Lord! You saved my life.

Kate scooted backward on her bottom, finally confident enough to try to stand. Only one problem. Her clothes were now damp and so cold. Straightening her legs was tough. And her feet suddenly ached. "Lord, just a few more minutes," she whispered. "I have to find a safe place."

Struggling against the strong wind, she kept her balance. Kate tried her cell phone once more. No signal. Determined to succeed, she turned toward the right. *I can do all things through Christ who strengthens me. I can do all things through Christ who strengthens me.*

For whatever reason, she thought about Phillip and her science project. Suddenly—with her life in jeopardy—it seemed so silly to hold a grudge against someone else. Really, the only thing that mattered right now was getting help for Sydney!

After a few treks through the deepening snow, Kate finally caught a glimpse of something red in the distance. "Oh, good!"

An old, dilapidated barn stood alone against the backdrop of white snow.

It's a long way away, but I think we can make it.

She used her own footprints to run back to Sydney. Kate found her in tears, seated on the ground next to a tree.

"I've found a safer place to wait," Kate explained. "Do you think you can take a few steps with my help, as long as they're not downhill?"

"I can do all things through Christ who strengthens me," Sydney spoke above the rising winds. "That was our Bible verse a couple of weeks ago in Sunday school."

"Wow! That's amazing! I was just quoting that verse!"

With Kate's help, Sydney rose and leaned against her. Together they took their first step through the mounds of snow.

"I can do all things through Christ who strengthens me," Sydney said.

"I can do all things through Christ who strengthens me," Kate echoed.

They continued saying the words until they drew closer, closer, closer to the old red barn. Finally they reached the door.

"It looks really old, Kate," Sydney said. "I don't even think that door will open. The hinges are broken."

"It *has* to open. It just has to." Kate reached for the door, praying all the time. After a struggle, she managed to get it open. "There! See!"

"Oh, it's dark in here." Sydney took a few hobbling steps inside, and Kate followed her.

"I wish we had a flashlight. It's kind of creepy."

"You don't think there are any. . ." Sydney's voice trailed off.

"What?" Kate asked.

"Rats?" Sydney whispered.

Kate shuddered. "Oh, I didn't think of that. How strange would that be? To find rats here."

She squinted, her eyes finally getting adjusted to the dark. "Ooo! This place is filled with spiderwebs!"

She found herself caught in one and began to bat at it, pulling it apart. "Gross!"

"This is so creepy!" Sydney said. "I don't like spiders any more than I do rats. But this place is filled with them. Look!" She pointed as a large spider crawled up the wall. "Remember your Aunt Molly said the creamery had spiders, too? I wonder if they were this big?"

"I don't know. But, look, Sydney. There are some mounds of hay over there." Kate pointed, getting more excited by the minute. "If we can get down inside the hay, I think we'll warm up. Then I'll try to use my phone again."

The girls had just settled down into the soft, cushy straw, when Kate thought she saw the door crack open. "W–who is it?" she called out. She began to shake all over!

The door slammed shut, making a clacking noise as the wind caught it and pushed it back and forth.

"Do you think that was a person?" Sydney asked. "Or maybe just the wind?"

"I'm too scared to look!" Kate pinched her eyes shut and sat in fear for a moment. Then, just as quickly, she felt courageous. "I'm tired of being a scaredy-cat! I'm going to look." She ran over to the door and inched it open. Staring out onto the open expanse of snow, she thought she caught a glimpse of someone.

"Come and help us!" she called out.

The person—who looked like a boy or maybe even a man—disappeared in the distance. He wore a dark jacket and carried a big backpack. But why would he be hanging out at an empty, abandoned barn? And what was in the backpack?

Or was he even real? Kate turned back to Sydney and sighed.

"Who was it?" her friend asked.

"I don't know." Kate rubbed at her eyes. "Maybe it was no one! Have you ever heard of a mirage?"

"A mirage?" Sydney yawned. "Like, something you see only in your imagination, but it seems so real you actually think it *is* real?"

"Right." Kate shrugged. "First it looked like someone. . . then it didn't. Maybe my overactive imagination is working overtime! My mom accuses me of that sometimes."

With the door still cracked, Kate opened the phone and saw a tiny signal. The GPS tracking system opened, but the signal faded almost immediately. Kate prayed a silent prayer: *Lord, I'm scared. And I don't know what to do. But I know You do. Help us, Lord. Please! I'm starting to imagine things—and they're not good!*

"My ankle hurts even more." Sydney's voice sounded weak. "And I'm getting so tired. Feels like it's nighttime, but it's barely even noon. Right?"

"Right. But I'm getting sleepy, too," Kate agreed with a yawn. "Maybe it's because it's so dark in here." She walked back over to the straw and curled up next to Sydney. She wanted to rest, but visions of spiders and spiderwebs kept her awake. What if she dozed off and one of those creepy crawlers crawled into her hair? Or down her arm! Ooo! What a terrible thought!

Minutes later, Kate's eyes grew heavier, heavier, heavier. Though she tried to fight the sleepiness, before she realized it, her eyes were closing—and she was sound asleep. She dreamed of rats and spiders, all chasing her down a big hill!

Kate couldn't be sure how much time passed, or if she was dreaming. But at some point, she heard the sound of a man's voice outside the barn and the sound of a dog barking. It sounded like a distant echo, like something from a dream.

"W–what is that?" She sat up, trying to figure out where she was. She could only make out shadows in the dark barn, but she definitely heard sounds coming from outside. The barking continued, sounding more and more familiar!

"Biscuit!" Was she dreaming? It sounded like her canine companion!

"Is anyone in there?" a man's booming voice rang out.

Kate jumped up, her eyes still heavy with sleep.

"Sydney! They've found us."

Sydney awakened and rubbed her eyes. "W—what? Who's found us?"

"Sounds like Pop and Uncle Ollie!" Kate tried to stand but could hardly move, she was so cold. Every joint and muscle ached.

"We're in here!" she called out. "Help us, please!"

"We're here! We're here!" Sydney called out, sounding hoarse and tired.

The door to the barn swung wide, and Kate's father stood there. Uncle Ollie appeared next to him with Biscuit at his side. The dog ran straight for Kate, jumping into the pile of hay and spreading it everywhere.

"Kate!" her father called out, his voice cracking with emotion. "I was so scared!"

"Pop! I'm so glad you're here! How did you know where to find us? I couldn't use my phone."

"Michael came and got us," Uncle Ollie explained. "He told us you were here."

"Michael?" Kate and Sydney spoke at the same time.

"How did he know we were here?" Kate asked, more confused than ever.

Uncle Ollie shrugged. "I'm not sure. He just said he saw you girls go into the old red barn on the south side of the pass. He was worried you might be in trouble."

"We *were* in trouble, so why didn't he come inside and talk to us?" Sydney asked. "That doesn't make any sense! He left us all by ourselves."

Uncle Ollie shrugged. "I don't know. I just know that he saved your lives by telling us you were here! We owe him our thanks."

"Humph." Sydney crossed her arms and made a face.

Biscuit jumped up and down, licking Kate in the face.

"He's happy to see you!" Uncle Ollie said with a nod.

"I'm happy to see him, too. I. . .I wasn't sure I ever would again." Kate burst into tears at once, realizing just how scared she'd been.

"How will we get back to the inn?" Sydney asked, looking nervous. "My ankle is injured. And I think it's really bad this time." Her tears started up again.

"Oh, we're on the snowmobiles," Kate's father explained. "But if you're injured, we'd better take you to the emergency room as soon as we get back to town."

Sydney's tears started flowing when she heard the words *emergency room*. "I'm never going to get to ski in the competition now. I can't believe this!"

"Remember, 'all things work together for good to them that love God, to them who are called according to his purpose,'" Uncle Ollie reminded her. "God will use this situation in a good way. Just watch and see."

"I don't see how He can, but I'm going to choose to believe that," Sydney said with a sigh.

Minutes later the girls climbed aboard the snowmobiles. Kate rode behind her father, and Sydney rode behind Uncle Ollie. As they made their way up one hill and down another, Kate thought about everything that had happened that day. Sydney's ankle. Almost falling down into a frozen creek. Finding refuge in a barn. Michael.

Hmm. Thinking of Michael raised so many questions. He hadn't been a mirage after all. But why didn't he stop to talk to them? Why did he run off, even if it was to get help?

Something about that boy just seems wrong.

As soon as they arrived at the inn, Kate's mother and Aunt Molly ran out to greet them. The girls were showered with kisses, then Kate's mom called Sydney's mother on the phone to tell her what had happened.

She gave them permission to take Sydney to the emergency room, and the girls and Mrs. Oliver piled into the car. As soon as they got inside the car, Kate finally felt free to cry. Oh, what a day it had been! Her tears flowed— partly in relief for being safe and partly because of the things she had faced earlier in the day.

Just then, her cell phone beeped. *Now I get a signal!* She glanced down, noticing a text message had come in from Elizabeth. Strangely, it was a scripture verse, the same one she and Sydney had been quoting all day.

Kate almost cried as she read the words: "I CAN DO ALL THINGS THROUGH CHRIST JESUS WHO STRENGTHENS ME."

Somehow she knew this was more than a coincidence.

Curds and Whey

Later that evening, after returning from the emergency room, Kate and Sydney enjoyed a quiet evening with the family. Thankfully, Sydney's ankle wasn't broken, though the doctor said it was a bad sprain. After putting a splint on it, he warned Sydney to stay off of it for at least two weeks and to keep it elevated. She didn't care for that idea very much.

"That's my whole Christmas break!" she had argued. Still, she had no choice. Under Aunt Molly's watchful eye, Sydney kept it elevated for the rest of the day and kept ice packs on it. Every time she started to put it down, Aunt Molly would tell her she was going to call her mama. Then Sydney would put it back up again and groan.

As they ate their dinner, Kate kept thinking about the skiing competition. What a shame! Three hundred dollars lost! Sydney wouldn't get to go on her mission trip now, after all. But what could be done about it? And with Sydney's ankle in such bad shape, would they ever figure out what was going on at the creamery? Surely Kate's parents wouldn't let her go alone to snoop, not after what happened today!

After a wonderful meal, everyone relaxed around the fireplace and told stories. Kate told everything that had happened to them on the ski course, right down to the point where she almost fell into the frozen creek. Her mother's eyes filled with tears.

"Oh, I should have gone with you! I can't believe I let you go without an adult. Can you ever forgive me for letting you go alone?"

Kate rushed to her mom's side and leaned against her. "There's nothing to forgive, Mom! We wanted to go by ourselves, remember? But I forgive you, anyway. . .if it makes you feel better! I've learned to forgive quickly and not to hold a grudge!" She gave her mom a squeeze. "Not that I could ever hold a grudge against you—even if you did do something wrong, which you didn't!"

"Thank you, sweetie," her mother said, giving her a kiss on the forehead. "That makes me feel better."

"Forgiving quickly is always a good plan," her father said. "Remember that time I had to forgive the man who claimed he invented one of my robots?"

"Oh, that's right," Kate said. "I'd forgotten about that."

"And remember the time that woman backed out of her parking space and hit my car?" Kate's mom said. "She wasn't very nice about it, and neither was the insurance company—but I had to forgive."

"I remember it was tough—especially because she wasn't nice about it." Kate shook her head, wondering how some people could be so mean. *Why can't everyone just be nice. . .like my mom and dad?*

"Once, someone found my checking account number and stole some money from my bank account," Uncle Ollie said. "He took hundreds of dollars and I was really mad. At first. But I got over it. I read that verse about forgiving as Jesus forgives and decided it wasn't worth holding a grudge."

"It never is," Aunt Molly said. She turned to Kate with a wink. "And I'm sure you've already forgiven the boy in your class who made fun of you, haven't you, honey?"

"Yes." Kate nodded. "I've forgiven him."

Sydney groaned and everyone looked her way.

"What's wrong?" Kate's mom asked with a worried look on her face. "Are you in pain?"

"No." Sydney looked sad. "I guess I just have to learn to forgive myself. I got so excited, thinking I could win that contest, that I put all my hopes in myself instead of in God. And I let myself down by getting hurt."

"You can hardly be mad at yourself for getting hurt!" Aunt Molly said. "That just doesn't make sense!"

"Oh, I know. But I'm disappointed in myself because I was *so* sure I was going to win the prize." Sydney shrugged. "Just goes to show you I was putting my trust in the wrong person. Me." She looked at the floor, her eyes filling with tears. "I guess I do that a lot, actually. I'm pretty good at sports, so sometimes I think I can do things on my own without God's help. I forget that He's the one in charge."

"I think we all do that sometimes," Uncle Ollie admitted. "But God always forgives us, if we ask."

"I will. I promise." Sydney smiled. "And if He wants me to go on that mission trip, I'll go—one way or the other."

"That's right! He always makes a way where there seems to be no way," Kate's dad said. "That's a promise from the Bible. And you know God's promises are true. He is faithful to do what He says He's going to do."

Sydney nodded and smiled for the first time all evening. "I feel so much better. Thank you for reminding me. I needed to hear that!"

Kate didn't say anything, but she was glad for the reminder, too.

After dinner, they all gathered in the big central room, where they ate large slices of warm apple pie and drank apple cider flavored with cinnamon sticks. As Kate leaned back against the super-sized pillows on the sofa, she looked around the room and thanked God for the special people in her life. She also thanked Him for protecting her and getting her back to her family safely.

For a moment—a brief moment—she felt a little sad. After all, they only had three more days in Mad River Valley. She and Sydney hadn't solved the mystery, and now Sydney wasn't going to get to ski. Looked like things weren't working out the way they'd hoped. Still, she had to believe God would work everything together for His good, just like Uncle Ollie said.

"A penny for your thoughts, Kate," Aunt Molly said with a hint of a smile.

Kate turned to her with a grin. "Oh, I'm just thinking of how God always has bigger and better plans than we do!"

"He sure does!" Aunt Molly agreed. "And I have a sneaking suspicion He's got more plans ahead than you know!"

Kate thought about that. Maybe Aunt Molly was right. Maybe there were plenty of adventures ahead!

A couple of hours later everyone headed off to bed.

"It's been a long day," Aunt Molly said with a yawn. "I'm going to sleep like a bug in a rug tonight."

"Ooo! Did you have to say that?" Kate said. "Thinking of bugs reminds me of all those spiders we saw today in that old barn!"

"Sorry, kiddo," said Aunt Molly. "I'm going to sleep well tonight."

"I'm not sleepy at all," Kate admitted. "My mind is still going, going, going! I can't seem to stop thinking about everything."

"Well, try to get some rest anyway, honey," her mother said. "You need to enjoy our last few days in Vermont, and that won't happen if you don't get enough sleep."

Kate and Sydney dressed for bed and then climbed

under the covers. Kate tossed and turned for at least an hour. She finally gave up and kicked off the blanket.

"What's up?" Sydney asked, opening one eye.

"It doesn't matter how hard I try, I just can't go to sleep," Kate said with a loud sigh.

"How come?" Sydney asked with a yawn.

"I have too much on my mind. Things are all jumbled up."

"Really? What do you mean?"

"My thoughts must look kind of like the curds and whey in that big container at the creamery. Everything is all mixed up. Lumpy."

Sydney chuckled. "Sounds funny, but I'm not really sure what you're talking about."

"Well, I have a lot on my mind. The competition. The creamery. The picture of that rat. The woman in the white coat. . .and her husband. Michael and the barn filled with spiders." She shook her head. "It's just a lot to think about. I'm having trouble falling asleep with my mind whirling like this."

"Well, try counting sheep," Sydney suggested.

Kate pulled the blanket back up and closed her eyes, but for some reason, all she saw were rats and spiders. "Ugh!" She tried to fall asleep with her eyes open, but that didn't work, either. Suddenly, Kate sat up in the bed and gasped. "Sydney! I just remembered something!"

Sydney rolled over in the bed and groaned. "We're never going to get any sleep!"

"I know, but this is important!"

"What is it?"

"The man behind the creamery. . .the one with the woman in the white coat. . ."

"What about him?" Sydney asked with a yawn.

"His name was *Mark*." Kate pushed the covers back once more, suddenly very nervous. "Remember? The woman called him by that name!"

"So?"

"So, Alexis said *Mark* was the name of the man who owns Cheese De-Lite, Mad River's main competitor. Right?"

"Ah." Sydney sat up in the bed. "That's right. And didn't she say his picture was on the Web site?"

"Yes, I think so. There's only one way to know for sure!"

The girls sprang from the bed and tiptoed out into the great room of the inn, where Uncle Ollie kept two computers for guests to use. Kate quickly signed online and typed in "CHEESE DE-LITE." When the Web page came up, she gasped.

"Oh, Sydney, look!" She pointed at the screen. Right there—in living color—was a professional photo of the man and the woman they'd seen on the tour that day, and again behind the creamery. "Mark and Abigail Collingsworth, owners of Cheese De-Lite in central Vermont." Kate shook her head as she read the words aloud. "Do you think they. . ."

"I don't know." Sydney began to pace back and forth. "I

suppose it's possible. Maybe they want to make Mad River Creamery look bad so they can steal their customers."

"Seems weird." Kate thought about it. "Why would they go to such trouble? Why not just hire an advertising firm to come up with better commercials or something?" She began to list several different possibilities, but none of them made sense.

"I don't know." Sydney shrugged.

Kate shook her head and continued to stare at the photo. "I just have the strangest feeling about these two. I can't put my finger on it."

"What are you thinking?" Sydney asked. "Tell me. . .please!"

Just then a light snapped on in the room. "What in the world are you girls doing up after midnight?"

Kate turned when she heard her dad's voice. "Oh, Dad, I'm sorry! We didn't mean to wake you up, but we just found another piece to the puzzle!"

All of the noise woke up Biscuit, who began to yap and run in circles. Before long, Uncle Ollie came into the room. Then Kate's mom. Then Aunt Molly. Then Dexter, who rubbed his eyes and looked at them all like he thought it was morning.

"What's happening, girls?" Aunt Molly said, rubbing the sleep from her eyes.

Kate turned her attention to the Web site, showing it to the others.

"Do these people look familiar to you?" she asked.

"Not at all." Aunt Molly squinted. "Wish I had my glasses on. . .I'd be able to see better. But they don't look familiar to me. What about you, Ollie? Do you know these folks?"

"I don't recognize them." He snapped his fingers. "But, come to think of it, I did hear Michael say some couple was snooping around town, asking a lot of questions about the creamery."

"Michael said that?" Kate released a breath, then leaned back in her chair.

"Yes."

Even stranger. "This is Mark Collingsworth," Kate explained, pointing at the picture of the man. "And his wife, Abby."

"What about them?" Aunt Molly asked.

"They own a creamery about fifty miles away. A competitor. This is the man Sydney and I saw the other day behind the building. And this woman was with him."

"Wow. Very suspicious." Uncle Ollie nodded. "We'll have to call the Hamptons in the morning and tell them." He scratched his bald head and pursed his lips. "Do you think he and his wife are the ones sabotaging the creamery?"

Kate sighed. "Maybe. I'm not sure. We don't really have any proof, and I hate to accuse someone unless I know for sure."

"We just know they were doing something behind the

building that day," Sydney added.

"Well, let's talk about this in the morning," Kate's dad said with a yawn. "There's no point trying to solve a mystery in the middle of the night. We all need our rest, especially if we're going to go to the Winter Festival."

Kate's heart twisted at his words. If Sydney couldn't compete, what was the point in going?

Just as the girls crawled back into bed once more, Sydney sat up with a silly grin on her face. "I have a brilliant-beyond-brilliant idea!"

"What is it?" Kate asked, yawning.

"Just because *I* can't enter the competition doesn't mean *you* can't."

"W—what?" Kate sat straight up and stared at her friend in disbelief. "Did you just say what I thought you said? You want me to take your place in the competition?"

"Sure! Why not? You did a great job skiing down the Rat. And I'd be willing to bet the people in charge of the festival will transfer my entry fee to you once they hear that I'm injured."

"But, why?"

"Because. . ." Sydney took her hand and gently squeezed it. "I think it would be good for you. For ages now I've heard you say you're no good at sports. I really think you would do a great job and it would prove—once and for all—that you can overcome your fear of sports."

"But. . .a competition?" Kate shivered just thinking

about it. "That's not the best place to prove something to myself."

"Don't you see, Kate?" Sydney said. "The only person you'd be competing against is yourself. This wouldn't have to be about anyone else. Just you. Face your fears head-on like I did. Ski down that mountain and you'll be a winner, no matter how fast you go. See what I'm saying?"

"I guess so." Kate pulled the covers up and leaned back against her pillows. "But I'll have to pray about it. I just don't know yet. I'll let you know in the morning, okay?"

"Okay." Sydney chuckled. "But get ready, Kate! I have a feeling you're going to be skiing tomorrow afternoon."

As Kate closed her eyes, she tried to picture herself sailing down a mountain. For some reason, every time she thought about it, she pictured Michael. . .whizzing by her, going a hundred miles an hour.

Thinking of Michael made her wonder—once again—why he'd been at the old spider-filled barn. Just a coincidence, or were there darker forces at work? And why had he left them there without saying a word? Very strange, even for him!

Kate's eyes grew heavy and she finally drifted off to sleep, dreaming dreams of red barns, snow-covered mountains. . .and rats. Big, hairy rats.

CHAPTER 12

Racing the Rat

Kate stood at the top of the hill, staring down. Somewhere between her middle of the night conversation with Sydney and now, she had decided to do it. She'd entered the skiing competition. And now, looking at the steep hill below, she was finally ready to face her biggest fear. "I can do this! I can do all things through Christ Jesus who strengthens me!"

Off in the distance, she heard Sydney's voice calling out. "Go, Inspector Gadget! Ski the Rat!"

"You can do it, honey." Her mother's voice echoed across the packed snow.

"Join the Rat Pack!" Uncle Ollie threw in his two cents' worth.

Hearing the words *The Rat Pack* reminded Kate that they hadn't yet solved the mystery about the creamery. Thinking about the creamery made her think of the woman in the white coat and the man with the sour expression on his face. Thinking of the man and woman reminded her of the day she and Sydney had hidden behind the Dumpster. And for some reason, thinking of the Dumpster reminded her of Bailey and how her phone rang at just the right—er, *wrong*—time.

"Why am I thinking about that right now?" Kate scolded herself. "I'm supposed to be getting ready to ski, not solve a crime!"

She took her place and tried to prepare herself the best she could.

"I can't believe I'm doing this. I can't believe I'm doing this!" Kate bent her knees and looked down at the long, slender skis. "Lord," she prayed, her eyes now closed, "help me get to the bottom without falling. Oh, and Lord, if You could help me win, I promise to use the money to bless somcone else!"

She opened her eyes and looked at the hill below. "It's just a hill. And I'm just like a little robot, about to glide from the top of the hill to the bottom. No big deal! What am I so worried about?"

Of course, there was that part where hundreds of people were watching her, but once she got started, she wouldn't have time to even think about them. No, all she had to think about was getting to the bottom without falling!

At the *pop* of the starter's pistol, Kate dug her poles into the snow and pushed off. As she began to sail down the hill, the cold wind whipped at her face. In fact, the wind was so strong it nearly knocked her down a time or two. Thankfully she managed to stay on her feet!

She came to the first curve and bent her knees, leaning into it. "C'mon, Snow-Bot!" she whispered. "You can do this!"

Kate managed to straighten out her position after making the curve. . .without falling! "Woo-hoo!" she called out to no one but the wind. "I did it!" Up ahead she saw a sharp curve to the left. "Uh-oh." She whispered another prayer, then bent her knees to make it around the turn.

Picking up speed, she almost lost control. After a bit of wobbling, she sailed on down, down, down. The trees off in the distance seemed to fly by, their snow-covered branches nothing but a blur.

For a moment, she remembered what had happened yesterday. . .how Sydney had injured her ankle in that very spot. How Kate had searched for a trail through those trees to find help. How they'd ended up in an old red barn with spiders. How Michael was there with his backpack on.

Michael. Hmm.

"Don't think about that right now!" Kate whispered to herself. "Just stay focused! Stay focused!"

After a couple more twists and turns, the bottom of the hill was in sight. Kate crouched a bit, trying to get more speed.

"C'mon, c'mon!" With faster speed than ever, she soared over the finish line, then—like a good robot would do—turned her feet to come to an abrupt stop. Kate's heart raced a hundred miles an hour.

"I did it! I did it!" She pulled off her goggles and began to cheer at the top of her lungs. She could hear the roar of the crowd and felt a little embarrassed. Kate put her hands over her mouth and giggled. Making it to the bottom without falling felt so good! And Sydney was right! She *had* proven something to herself.

I'm not bad at sports! I need to stop saying that!

One by one, she watched the other skiers in her age group. A couple of them fell. One of them made it all the way to the bottom, but didn't seem to be moving as fast. One girl was really, really good. Kate watched her as she came sailing down the hill. Her bright blue snowsuit stood out against the bright white snow.

"Wow, she looks like a pro." At the very last minute, the girl lost control of her skis and went sprawling in the snow.

"Oh man! I hope she's okay," Kate whispered.

Thankfully, the girl rose to her feet and raised her hand to show everyone she wasn't injured. Everyone cheered and she skied down to the bottom of the hill and took a bow.

Finally it was Michael's turn. Kate had almost forgotten he was competing until she saw him. She could hear Uncle Ollie's cheers off in the distance.

Michael is really blessed to have Uncle Ollie in his life. He needs someone like that to support him.

Michael started off well and even made the first curve with no problem. But then, at the second big turn, he almost lost his footing. Thankfully, he didn't fall, but it did slow him down a little. He still skied very well, and Kate knew he'd made up for the lost time. At least, it seemed like it! She was surprised when she saw his time come up on the board. *Oh wow. It took him almost a full second longer to reach the bottom than me. Weird.*

Only one skier was left. Kate watched as the boy sailed down the hill like a professional skier.

"Wow, he's so good!" She watched in awe as he gracefully moved back and forth on his skis. Then, just before he reached the final turn, his skis somehow bumped up against each other and he toppled over! A loud gasp went up from the crowd.

"Oh, that's terrible!" Kate covered her eyes, not wanting to look. Hopefully he wasn't badly hurt.

It took a couple of minutes for him to stand, but he finally managed. The crowd applauded his efforts, and he responded with a dramatic bow. Kate laughed. *He's a great sport!*

After that, everything seemed to move in slow motion. Kate heard her name announced over the loudspeaker. "The winner of this year's Winter Festival junior level competition is twelve-year-old Kate Oliver from Philadelphia, Pennsylvania!"

It almost felt like they were calling someone else's name.

"Me?" she whispered. "I won?" Kate could hardly believe it! The whole thing seemed impossible. . .like a dream. Only this *wasn't* a dream! It was true. Every bit of it!

An older man gestured for her to come to the stage, which she did with shaking knees. She climbed a few stairs and stood before the people.

"Kate Oliver, congratulations on skiing the Rat! You're now an official member of the Rat Pack!" He handed her a T-shirt and opened it to show the icky-looking rat on the back.

Kate giggled and took the shirt. "Thank you so much!" She searched for Uncle Ollie in the crowd. When she found him, she held up the shirt and grinned.

"The Winter Festival of Mad River Valley is proud to give you this trophy for your performance today." The man standing next to Kate gave her a big silver trophy with two skis on top. "And of course. . ." the man continued, handing her a check, "the grand prize of three hundred dollars!"

Kate gripped the check in her hand and whispered a prayer. "Oh, thank You, Lord! I know just what to do with this!"

The crowd started applauding, and Kate felt her cheeks warm up. They always did that when she was embarrassed. No doubt they were as red as tomatoes!

She looked through all of the people till she found her family and Sydney standing off to the left of the stage. Getting down the stairs was the easy part. Making her way through the crowd—with so many people patting her on the back and saying congratulations—was a lot harder than she imagined!

Finally she saw her mother. "Oh, Kate! You were wonderful! Congratulations! We're so proud of you!"

"I knew you could do it!" her dad hollered.

The others in her family gathered around, looking at the trophy. Kate held it up for all to see.

"She's a beauty!" Uncle Ollie said.

"That's the coolest trophy I've ever seen!" Dexter added.

"Wonderful, wonderful!" Aunt Molly added. "I'm tickled pink, honey. And even more tickled that you were wearing my old skis! What an honor!"

Biscuit jumped up and down in excitement. Kate reached down to scratch him behind the ears. "I know, boy! You're so excited!"

Sydney came hobbling toward her on her sore ankle. "Oh, Kate! I'm so proud of you! You're the fastest skier here."

Kate shook her head. "I still don't know how it's possible. And I know for a fact that your time would have been better than mine, if only. . ." She looked down at her friend's ankle and sighed.

"No *if onlys* today," Sydney said with a happy nod. "Today we're *all* winners."

Off in the distance, Michael walked by, his shoulders slumped forward in defeat. Kate noticed the sour look on his face. He looked her way and glared at her.

Wow. Not everyone is acting like a winner, Kate thought.

He reached underneath the stage and pulled out his

backpack, but as he started to put it on, something fell out of it. Something small. And furry.

"Is that what I think it is, or is my imagination acting up again?" Kate whispered.

At once, Biscuit went crazy! He ran toward the small fuzzy critter, barking like a maniac. Only when Kate took a second look, did she realize for sure just what she was looking at! Right away, she began to scream!

"It's. . .it's. . .a. . .*rat!*"

The Mouse Takes the Cheese

As soon as Kate shouted, Michael dropped his backpack into the snow and began to run away from the crowd. Kate had never seen anyone move that fast! He shot through the throng of people, heading toward the lodge.

"Oh, I wish I could run!" Sydney said, wringing her hands together. "This bum ankle of mine won't let me!"

Kate raced after Biscuit, who now stood at the edge of the snow barking like a maniac. She couldn't blame him! *Did I really see what I thought I saw? Did a rat. . .a real, live rat. . .just fall out of Michael's backpack?*

As she got closer to the stage, she glanced down to see what Biscuit held in his mouth. He yanked it around to the right, then the left, then the right, then the left.

"Oh, gross! If it was a rat, it's a goner now!" Kate didn't want to touch it. *Oh, how disgusting!*

A crowd gathered around. "Look, everyone!" Dexter shouted. "Biscuit caught a rat. Good boy!"

"A rat?" one man said with a smirk on his face. "How ironic!"

It took Kate a minute to realize what he meant. They were standing at the bottom of the Rat ski course, after all.

People began to laugh, but Kate didn't feel like joining them. Not yet, anyway. She had a sinking feeling.

"Look!" another man called out. "This dog is going crazy!"

Biscuit continued his chewing and chomping frenzy, and Kate actually felt sorry for the poor little rat. What a terrible way to die!

She grabbed the dog by his collar and scolded him. "Biscuit, let go! Stop! Enough already!"

After a couple of seconds, he finally dropped the furry little thing. Kate gasped when she looked down and saw. . . metal pieces? *Metal pieces inside a rat? What?*

"What is that?" Sydney hobbled up beside her.

"Oh, wow, Kate!" Sydney looked shocked. "It's not a real rat at all. It's a little. . ."

"Robot," Kate whispered. "It's a robotic rat! No wonder it ran in crazy circles that day at the creamery. And no wonder McKenzie couldn't find a photo of another rat that looked like this one. It's not real. It never was." Relief swept over her. "That means they never really had a rat infestation at the creamery. Not real rats, anyway. Just robotic ones. But why? Why would Michael do this?"

Uncle Ollie reached down into the snow to pick up the robotic rat, which Biscuit had almost destroyed. He rolled it from one hand to another, looking it over. "I don't believe this. I really don't believe this. I'm the one who taught him how to build robots, but I never dreamed he would take the things I'd taught him and use them to hurt someone!"

"There were three rats that first day at the creamery," Sydney said, reaching for Michael's backpack. "So there must be at least two more inside!" She looked up at Uncle Ollie. "Is it okay to open it and look inside to see?"

"I give you permission." Michael's mother, Maggie, drew near. "We need to know for sure before. . ." Her eyes filled with tears, and Kate suddenly felt very sorry for her.

Poor woman! She's still sad about her dad dying, and now this!

Mr. and Mrs. Hampton walked up. They both looked completely shocked.

Sydney reached inside the backpack and came out with not just one but two furry critters! As soon as she saw them, she began to scream. "Ooo! More rats!"

One of them flew up into the air, then hit the ground. Kate reached down and grabbed it. "But they're not real. See?" She rolled it around in her hand. "I can feel the metal parts inside. And look, here's where the batteries go." She showed everyone the belly of the rat.

By now, several people had gathered.

"Step back, everyone!" Mr. Hampton said, drawing near. "Step back!"

He approached Kate and took the rats from her, examining them carefully. "Whose bag is this?" he asked, pointing to the backpack.

"It belongs to my son, Michael," Maggie said with tears in her eyes.

"Where did he go?" Mr. Hampton looked around. "Is he still here?"

"I saw him running toward the lodge," an older woman said. "He was going mighty fast!"

Mr. Hampton and Uncle Ollie led the way to the lodge. Kate and her family trudged along behind him in the snow. Kate prayed all the way. *Lord, please let Michael still be there. And help us understand why he would do something like this to the Hamptons!*

As they entered the main room of the lodge, Kate saw Michael sitting in front of the fireplace. As soon as he heard everyone come in the door, he turned and looked their way. Kate couldn't help but notice he had tears in his eyes.

What's up with that? What secrets are you hiding, Michael?

Mr. Hampton walked straight over to him and dropped the backpack down on the floor. "Is this yours, son?"

"Yes, sir." Michael looked down at the ground.

"And these, um, rats. They're yours?" Mr. Hampton continued.

Michael hung his head in shame. "Yes, sir. I made them. In my basement."

Maggie walked to his side and slipped an arm over his shoulder. "Michael, we just need the truth. Are you the one who. . ." Her voice cracked. "Are you the one who put the rats in the creamery?"

Kate's heart twisted as he gave a slow nod and then began to cry.

Why would he do such a thing? That's horrible!

Michael turned to Uncle Ollie, talking a mile a minute. "You don't understand what they did to my grandpa!"

With an angry look on his face, he pointed to Mr. and Mrs. Hampton, who stood in silence listening to him. "My Grandpa Joe worked for them for years as a security guard. He was a good man. . ." Michael's voice cracked. "But they fired him! Fired him. For no good reason. He needed that job. We had bills to pay!"

Mr. Hampton looked stunned. "We had good reasons for firing him, Michael, whether you know it or not."

Michael shook his head, growing angrier by the moment. "After he lost his job, Grandpa started getting sick. I know it was because he was so depressed. He was never the same after that. And my mom had to work harder than ever to pay for his medical bills."

Michael began to shake uncontrollably. Kate watched as he clenched his fists.

"So you wanted to get even with them?" Uncle Ollie asked. "You sabotaged the creamery to get even?"

Michael nodded. "I. . .wanted to bring them down! They hurt my grandpa, and I wanted to hurt them!"

Ooo! Kate thought about the scripture she had learned

from Aunt Molly. *So that's what happens when you hold a grudge! People really do end up getting hurt!*

"What did you do, son?" Uncle Ollie asked. "Tell me everything."

"I. . .I went to the old barn on the south slope and got lots of spiders. I set them loose in the creamery. But I could tell that wasn't going to be enough to convince people, so I. . ." He shook his head, then stared at Uncle Ollie. "I used what you taught me about robots. Made three of them. Figured if I could. . ." He paused and shook his head. "I just wanted sales to go down at the creamery. I wanted to hurt the Hamptons like they hurt us!"

Michael's mother drew near and wrapped Michael in her arms. "Oh, honey," she spoke with tears in her eyes. "First of all, it's wrong to get even with people, even if they really do hurt you. But in this case, you're completely mistaken! The Hamptons are good people."

"No, they're not!" He looked at his mother like she was crazy.

"Oh, Michael, there's so much you don't know about your grandpa. He was a good man, but in those last few months before he lost his job, he was already very sick. The Hamptons didn't know it, of course. He didn't want them to know."

"What do you mean, Mom?"

"He told me he'd been falling asleep on the job. A lot. It was probably the medication he was on. I always suspected that, of course. And he never told the Hamptons he was on medicine for his weak heart, so they never knew. He didn't want anyone to know."

Geneva Hampton began to cry. "I always thought there was something more going on with Joe. He kept falling asleep on the job. But I didn't realize he was on medication!"

"He was," Maggie said. "And mighty strong medicine, at that." She turned back to Michael to finish the story. "One night your grandpa fell asleep on the job. It had happened before, but this time a fire broke out in the area where the cows were kept."

"I remember that night," Uncle Ollie said, scratching his head. "It was a close call! The Hamptons could have lost all of their cows that night."

"And it was your grandpa's fault," Maggie said softly to Michael.

Michael shook his head. "Why didn't you ever tell me this? Why did you let me think. . ." He looked up at Mr. and Mrs. Hampton and shook his head. "I just thought they were being mean to him. Now I don't know what to think."

"I think we're all confused and hurt," Uncle Ollie said. "And when we're hurt, we often do things we don't mean to do. I once heard a pastor say, 'Hurt people hurt people.' And it's so true."

Mr. Hampton shook his head, looking more than a little upset. "Oh, I feel terrible! I wish I had known about Joe's heart condition! We could have worked something out. Maybe cut back on his hours or something."

"No, he was really too frail to be working, anyway," Maggie said. "That's why I tried to pick up so many extra hours at the diner. I figured the more money I made, the less he would have to worry about finances. We were doing okay, until. . ."

"Until he had the heart attack?" Uncle Ollie asked.

Maggie nodded. "Yes. Then I knew. . ." She began to cry and Kate reached over to wrap her arms around her. "That's when I knew he would never work again. At that point, I just wanted to see him get better, to come back home."

"We just wanted everything to be. . .normal," Michael said, his eyes glistening with tears. "But then. . ."

"Well, we all know what happened next." Maggie sniffled then wiped her nose with a tissue. "He went to be with Jesus. And, of course, he's in heaven celebrating right now, but we still miss him so much."

"Enough to do some really dumb things." Michael kicked at a pile of snow with the toe of his tennis shoe. "I. . .I'm so sorry. I really thought you guys fired Gramps because. . .well, because you didn't like him."

"Oh no, honey!" Geneva Hampton wrapped her arms around his shoulders. "We loved your grandpa. And we were concerned about him. That's really why we let him go. Though he never told us about his illness, we knew something was wrong and we decided the job was putting too much stress on him."

"You did the right thing," Maggie said. "It wounded his pride a little, but he needed the rest."

Michael looked at Mr. Hampton with tears in his eyes. "Can you ever forgive me? I'm so sorry."

"Of course we forgive you, Michael," Mr. Hampton said. "It would be wrong to hold a grudge."

"I'll do everything I can to make this better," Michael said with a hopeful look in his eye. "I know! I'll come to work for you. You won't have to pay me or anything. I'll work in the factory every afternoon to make up for what I've done. And I'll tell everyone I know to buy Mad River Valley cheese!"

Mr. Hampton laughed. "Well, we can always use the help, but you're a little young to be working, aren't you?"

Michael shook his head. "I'm turning fifteen in a week! I can have a job if my mom says so, right? I just want to make up for what I've done. I. . .I can't believe I let my anger get control of me like that. Next time I'm going to wait till I have all of the facts before acting!"

"Great plan!" Mr. Hampton gave him a pat on the back. "Now, I have an idea! Geneva made a huge pot of cheddar cheese soup for the festival. It's out in the car. Are you folks hungry?"

"Cheddar cheese soup?" Kate's stomach rumbled, just thinking about it. Man, did that ever sound good!

She turned to Sydney with a smile on her face and

whispered, "I can't believe it! We were right! The creamery was being sabotaged!"

Just as quickly, she thought about the woman in the white coat and her husband. If Michael was the one who'd sabotaged the creamery, who were they. . .and what were they doing in Mad River Valley?

CHAPTER 14

Christmas in Vermont

On the day after the big Winter Festival, Kate went to church with her family. She knew their time in Vermont was drawing to a close, and she wanted to enjoy every moment. She couldn't have been more surprised to hear the preacher's topic of the day: forgiveness. What a fun coincidence. Of course, Aunt Molly called it a *God-incidence*. Kate couldn't help but agree!

A couple of times during the service, Kate looked at Maggie and Michael who sat in the row beside them. He really seemed to pay attention to the sermon. And she felt pretty sure he'd learned his lesson about forgiveness.

But, had *she*?

As soon as they arrived back at the inn, they all ate lunch together, then Aunt Molly and Kate's mother washed the dishes. Sydney settled into a chair across from Uncle Ollie to talk about sports, and Kate. . .well, Kate had something specific on her mind. There was something she needed to do. Something she should have done days before.

Heading over to Uncle Ollie's computer, she signed into

her e-mail account. Then, thinking carefully about each word, she began to type.

> *Dear Phillip,*
>
> *I'm in Mad River Valley, Vermont, on Christmas vacation with my family. I've been working on my science project. It's all about cheese! (Boy, have I learned a LOT!) I'm sure you're hard at work on your project back in Philly or wherever you're spending your vacation. Hope you're having fun!*
>
> *I just want you to know that I'm sorry if I ever did anything to make you feel like you're not as smart as me. I think you're so smart and should have told you so instead of always trying to make it look like I'm the best!*
>
> *When you made fun of my project a few weeks ago, it hurt my feelings, but I have forgiven you. Will you forgive me for the mean things I was thinking about you since then? Please? When I get back to school, I'm going to ask Mrs. Mueller if we can work together on our next project. The Bible says that one can put a thousand to flight but two can put ten thousand to flight. That's kind of a fancy way of saying we can do more if we work together!*

*I learned a lot about that this week in
Vermont. I worked with my friend Sydney
and together we accomplished great things.
I can't wait to tell you all about it! The rest
of the school year is going to be better if we're
friends!*

See you soon! Kate Oliver

She read over the e-mail once or twice, then pressed the
SEND button.

Just then, Kate heard her mother's voice behind her.
"What are you doing, honey? The others are waiting to
open Christmas presents!"

"Oh, just taking care of something I should have done
days ago." Kate turned around and smiled at her mom,
feeling contentment in her heart. "Forgiving someone. Or
rather, *letting* that someone know I've forgiven him!"

"Wow. Well, I can think of no greater Christmas gift
than that. You know, honey, God is in the forgiving business.
That's why He sent His Son, Jesus, as a baby in a manger. He
knew that we—His children—all needed a Savior."

Kate nodded. "I know. But I'm glad you reminded me. I'll
never look at the baby in the manger the same again, Mom!"

In the next room, Kate heard voices raised in song.
Aunt Molly warbled, "Deck the halls with boughs of holly"
at the top of her lungs, and the others soon joined in.

"Come and join us, honey," her mother said, extending

her hand. "We've got some celebrating to do. And lots of presents to open!"

"Yes, we do!" Kate thought about all of the victories of the past week as she made her way into the great room, where flames lit the fireplace and her family members sang in several keys at once! In one week's time she had solved a mystery, won a competition, and forgiven Phillip. *That's a lot, Lord!*

Only one thing left to do. . .and oh, what fun it was going to be! Talk about a merry Christmas!

One by one the family members opened presents. Kate was tickled to get so many fun gifts—a hand-knitted scarf from Aunt Molly, a great journal from Sydney, and lots of cool things from her mom and dad. Even Dexter gave her a great present—a cool new digital recorder.

Finally the moment arrived. . .the one Kate had been waiting for. She watched as Sydney opened the gift she had so carefully wrapped. Everyone's eyes nearly popped when they saw the three hundred dollars in cash inside.

"W–what?" Sydney looked at her, stunned. "What have you done, Kate?"

"It's my Christmas gift to you!" she exclaimed. "The *only* reason I agreed to take your place in the competition was to help you go on your mission trip. Of course, I never dreamed I would actually win. . .but I did! It was a huge blessing for both of us! Don't you see? Now you can go to Mexico."

"B—but. . .I didn't earn this money." Sydney tried to hand it back to her. "*You* did."

"No, the way I look at it, it's really a miracle I made it from the top of the Rat to the bottom without falling on my face and embarrassing myself in front of hundreds of people! So, we'll call that our miracle money. And I can think of no better way to spend my miracle money than on a mission trip!"

"A—are you sure?" Sydney stammered.

"Sure I'm sure! Take it. Go to Mexico. Have the time of your life." Kate leaned over and whispered, "Just don't have any big adventures without me, okay?"

"Okay! I'll try!" Sydney giggled and hugged the gift tightly. "Oh, I don't believe it! Can I call my mom? Would that be okay?"

"Of course, honey." Aunt Molly pointed to the phone. "You go right ahead. But the rest of us still have presents to open."

Sydney headed over to the phone to make the call. Kate could hear her squeals as she shared the story with her mother. Oh, how wonderful it felt. . .to be able to do something so fun for a friend!

Several minutes later, after everyone had opened all of the Christmas gifts, Kate heard singing at the door. At least, she *thought* it was singing. Sounded a little off-key to her!

"Sounds like carolers!" Uncle Ollie said.

He opened the door and Kate smiled as she saw Mr. and

Mrs. Hampton outside, along with Michael and his mother. Together, the four of them sang "The First Noel" really, really loud. Oh, what a wonderful sound, to hear their voices raised in harmony! A little off-key, but harmony, just the same!

Thank You, God! Kate giggled. *This is what happens when people forgive one another! You fix their broken relationships!*

After they finished singing, Aunt Molly invited them inside. "You're just in time!" she said. "We baked Snickerdoodles and I've made wassail! Let's celebrate together!"

"We have a lot to celebrate, don't we?" Mr. Hampton said, smiling at Michael. "God has done such wondrous things this Christmas season. He's brought us all closer together and given us plenty of reasons to look ahead to a bright new year!"

"Yes, He has," Mrs. Hampton agreed with a twinkle in her eye.

They had all settled into chairs around the dining room table to eat cookies and drink wassail when Mr. Hampton cleared his throat to get the attention of everyone in the room. "I have some news," he said, clasping his hands together.

Everyone looked his way. Kate could hardly wait to hear what he had to say. She hoped it was good news!

"Geneva and I are selling the creamery!" Mr. Hampton

grinned from ear to ear.

"W—what?" Everyone spoke in unison.

"Are you kidding?" Uncle Ollie asked.

"Please say this is a joke!" Aunt Molly added. "We don't want you to move away!"

"We're not moving away," he said. "I promise!"

"Oh, Mr. Hampton. . .please don't give up just because your sales are down right now," Michael begged. "I'll do anything. . .everything to help you get them up again."

Mr. Hampton laughed. "No, you don't understand. Geneva and I are ready to retire. And we have no children to pass the business to. God never blessed us with a son or a daughter. A wonderful couple from central Vermont has been talking with us about buying the place. In fact, I think you met them, girls. They were on the tour that day. . ."

"Abigail and Mark Collingsworth?" Kate stammered.

"Why, yes." Geneva Hampton looked stunned. "How did you know their names? That's amazing."

"Oh, trust me," Sydney said. "We know a lot more than that about them. They already own a creamery called Cheese De-Lite about fifty miles from here. They're Mad River's main competitors."

"Not anymore!" Geneva Hampton laughed. "They're moving their operation to Mad River Valley. From now on, there will be no Cheese De-Lite. But they will bring their signature cheese flavor with them. . .the low-fat version of cheddar."

"Low-fat cheese?" Kate wrinkled her nose. "No wonder that man has such a sour look on his face. That doesn't sound very yummy."

"No, he had a sour look on his face because he *really* thought we had rats at the creamery," Mrs. Hampton said with a laugh. "We had a hard time convincing him it wasn't true! But now that he knows the real story, he's made us an offer. And it's a good one. So the next time you see him, he will be smiling, I'm sure!"

"Still, low-fat cheese?" Kate said. "Icky!"

"Hey, we have to cut back on our calories every way we can!" Sydney said. After a sheepish look, she added, "Well, at least *I* do, if I'm going to be a sports star!"

Kate sighed. "I guess I'd better cut back on calories, too. Skiing was a lot of fun. You never know, I may end up liking sports, too! Wouldn't that be something!"

"I can hardly wait to tell the other Camp Club Girls!" Sydney laughed. "Can you imagine the look on Bailey's face when she hears you won a skiing competition!"

"And what about McKenzie! She's going to flip!" Kate chuckled, just thinking about it. "I'm excited to tell Elizabeth. I know she's been praying. I always feel better, knowing she's praying."

"Me, too," Sydney observed. "And I always feel better when I'm spending time with you. That's why. . ." Her eyes filled with tears. "That's why I'm so sad this week is almost over! We have to go home soon!"

"Let's spend every minute together. . .having fun!" Kate said.

A few minutes later, Michael asked if he could speak to Kate in private. She sat next to him on the couch wondering why he had such an embarrassed look on his face.

"You know, I bragged a lot about how fast I am on the slopes," he said.

"Yes, you did," Kate agreed. "But you *are* fast. I saw you with my own eyes."

"Yes, but I saw *you*, too! And you're amazing, Kate! Really amazing."

"You think so?" She felt her cheeks turn warm as an embarrassed feeling came over her.

"I know so." He grinned. "Are you coming back to Mad River Valley next winter? If so, I'd better start practicing now if I'm ever going to beat you."

Kate laughed long and loud at that one. "How funny! A boy actually thinks I'm good at sports! That's hysterical!" She giggled. "I don't know if I'll compete next year. I liked it more when I was skiing for fun. But I'm sure we'll come back for a visit if Aunt Molly and Uncle Ollie invite us!"

"Oh, you're *always* welcome!" Aunt Molly said, sweeping Kate into her arms. "Please come and see me as often as you like."

"Yes, I feel sure there are lots of mysteries to solve in

Mad River Valley," Uncle Ollie said.

"Like who ate all the Snickerdoodles when I wasn't looking," Maggie said, looking at Uncle Ollie.

"Or who put too much cheese in the fondue," Michael threw in.

"Or who used my treadmill when I wasn't looking!" Uncle Ollie added, looking at Sydney.

"Wasn't me!" Aunt Molly proclaimed.

They all laughed at that one.

"It doesn't matter where Kate goes, adventure always seems to follow," her dad said. "She's my little super-sleuth!"

"I just *love* adventure!" Kate said. "Love, love, love it!"

She and Sydney spent the next few minutes telling everyone about some of the cases they had solved with the Camp Club Girls. On and on their stories went, filling the ears of everyone in the room.

When she finished, her dad looked at her, beaming with pride. "I'm so proud of you, Kate."

"Here's to Inspector Gadget!" Sydney raised her glass of wassail.

Seconds later, everyone joined her, offering up a toast to Kate. She felt all warm and tingly inside. Solving mysteries made her feel good from the top of her head to the bottom of her toes.

But what made her feel even better—much, much better, in fact—was forgiving Phillip. Perhaps that had been the greatest lesson of all this week. Never again would she hold a grudge. No, from now on she would forgive. . . quickly!

"Be kind to one another, tenderhearted, forgiving one another, even as God in Christ forgave you." Kate smiled as she whispered the words. Yes, from now on, she would always be quick to forgive!

Aunt Molly stood and began to sing "Joy to the World." Uncle Ollie joined her, then Mr. and Mrs. Hampton. Before long, most everyone was singing, even Michael.

Sydney leaned over and whispered in Kate's ear. "We solved another case, Kate! Can you believe it?"

"Yep!" Turning to her friend, Kate whispered the words they loved so much: "Super-sleuths forever!"

Sydney winked and added, "Forever and ever!"

Kate nodded, then happened to look over at the little manger scene on the fireplace mantle. She focused on the babe inside, remembering what her mother had said. *He came to forgive*, she reminded herself.

With a *very* merry heart, Kate lifted her voice and began to sing!

CAMP CLUB GIRLS

books from BARBOUR PUBLISHING

AVAILABLE WHEREVER BOOKS ARE SOLD.